MAD DOG
MOONLIGHT

WITHDRAWN FROM
THE NEELB LIBRARY SERVICE

ON...

FOR SALE AT

Also by Pauline Fisk for Bloomsbury

SABRINA FLUDDE
THE RED JUDGE

WITHDRAWN FROM
THE NEELB LIBRARY SERVICE

ON.......................
FOR SALE AT

MAD DOG MOONLIGHT

Pauline Fisk

BLOOMSBURY

LONDON BERLIN NEW YORK

For Jake

Bloomsbury Publishing, London, Berlin and New York

First published in Great Britain in 2009 by Bloomsbury Publishing Plc
36 Soho Square, London, W1D 3QY

Copyright © Pauline Fisk 2009
The moral right of the author has been asserted

Original poem in Welsh by Lewis Glyn Cothi,
English version from George Borrow's *Wild Wales*

All rights reserved
No part of this publication may be reproduced or
transmitted by any means, electronic, mechanical, photocopying
or otherwise, without the prior permission of the publisher

A CIP catalogue record of this book is available from the British Library

ISBN 978 0 7475 9407 9

The paper this book is printed on is certified independently in
accordance with the rules of the FSC. It is ancient-forest friendly.
The printer holds chain of custody.

FSC
Mixed Sources
Product group from well-managed
forests and other controlled sources
Cert no. SGS - COC - 2061
www.fsc.org
© 1996 Forest Stewardship Council

Typeset by Dorchester Typesetting Group Ltd
Printed in Great Britain by Clays Ltd, St Ives plc

1 3 5 7 9 10 8 6 4 2

www.bloomsbury.com
www.paulinefisk.co.uk

'From high Plynlimmon's shaggy side
Three streams in three directions glide;
To thousands at their mouths who tarry
Honey, gold and mead they carry.
Flow also from Plynlimmon high
Three streams of generosity;
The first, a noble stream indeed,
Like rills of Mona runs with mead;
The second bears from vineyards thick
Wine to the feeble and the sick;
The third, till time shall be no more,
Mingled with gold shall silver pour.'

Lewis Glyn Cothi

North Eastern Educ. and Library Board	
NESSEC	
C40 0267827	
Askews	11-Aug-2009
JF	£6.99

CONTENTS

Mum's Story

Winter came early the year that you were born – and I mean early. Usually we'd be off back down the Preseli Mountains before the first storms blew in, making the high roads impossible to navigate. But that year the last leaves had scarcely dropped off the trees before the bad weather rolled in.

The main roads were clear, but the back roads up round Snowdonia and Plynlimon, and all about the region that people in the old days used to call the 'wilderness of Elynedd', were like sheets of ice. And, as you know, the wheels of our old van aren't that good at the best of times.

It was cold too. By God, it was cold. Usually it takes a whole winter to get through our supply of gas, but we were through the first two bottles already and only had one left.

I remember worrying about that. Lying in the van listening to your dad snoring and the wind howling outside as a snowstorm got up and flakes slid down the windows. All the blankets were piled on the bed but I was shivering. Usually a bit of bad weather doesn't bother me. I'll sleep through anything, me. It's being born with travellers' blood – that's what I say. The blood of people who are used to putting up with things.

But, blood or no blood, that night I couldn't sleep – and it was nothing to do with the weather. I was nearly nine months gone with you and, no matter how I lay, I couldn't get comfortable. There wasn't a bit of me that didn't ache, but my back was worst. Our mattress was old and its springs were giving out. We were always saying we were going to look out for another, but we'd never found one.

Worse than the mattress, though, was the small matter of you. You never liked it when I rested, you little mad dog, you. The moment I put my feet up, you'd start having a go. What you wanted was me on my feet walking up and down, rocking your impatient little body inside of me. I used to reckon that even in my womb your travellers' blood was driving you.

Anyhow, that night I got so fed up lying there being pummelled by you and snored at by your dad that I climbed out of bed, wrapped myself up in the nearest coat that I could find and went outside to stand in the snowstorm.

I've always liked doing that – not just watching the weather but feeling it going on all around me. Other people hide from it but I've always wanted to drink it up. There are songs to be heard in the dawn, you know, when the sun's getting up and the sky is thin and clear. And colours in a storm – you can see them before it ever hits. Reds, blues and greens that people never notice because they never look. A storm should never surprise you, not if you use your eyes.

Least, that's what I always used to think. But that night the storm surprised me, all right. It was ragged with snowflakes one minute, dancing at breakneck speed and churning up clouds like waves on a sea. Then, all of a sudden, it was gone. The moon blinked like an eye, opening and shutting, turning the landscape back and forth from silver to black as if a police car with flashing lights had arrived to move us on.

Then the clouds suddenly blew away like a carpet that had been rolled up. The wind dropped. The land stopped flashing on and off. The moon shone full. The stars were bright and between them all – I swear to God – A SILVER RIVER FLOWED THROUGH THE SKY.

I scarcely could believe it, and yet there it was. A real live river, made of silver, in the sky above our van! It snaked a path between the stars, and it was no Milky Way. No jet stream that I'd mistaken for something else, or strand of cloud lit up by the moon, or the Northern Lights or anything like that. It was a river of water flowing over my head, over the mountains and off through the night, and it was as real as anything I've ever seen. There were waves on it, and beaches on its shoreline, and pools that were still and deep, and other places where the water ran fast, bubbling and crashing in its hurry to get on.

At one and the same time it was just like any other river I'd ever seen, and yet as unlike any other river as anything could be. I remember calling for your dad, but he carried on snoring and didn't hear. I was the only one who saw it. I held out my hands as if I wanted to take hold of it. I'd have given anything to leap into those shining waters and let them carry me away. But they were too far from me and, besides, I had you to think of.

No sooner had the merest idea of swimming lodged itself in my head, than you got my insides, you crafty little beast, and started tying them in knots. And I'm not just talking about kicking here. I'm not even

3

talking about pummelling. I'm talking about going into labour.

From the first contraction onwards, you really went for it. The world was out there and you couldn't wait to see it. Nothing timid about your birth, my lad. Nothing nervous, inching forward. From that first contraction onwards, I was in for a full-on assault.

Hardly surprisingly, I forgot about the silver river and rushed to shake your dad awake. For the next couple of hours, it was panic stations. The mountain passes were all choked with snow, but then I didn't want to go to hospital anyway. I wanted you to be delivered on the open road the way that travelling people always used to do it. But, for all my forcing him to mug up on home deliveries, your dad had refused to hear of such a thing.

In the end, though, I had it my way. By the time your dad got the van even halfway down the mountain, the clouds had long-since come rolling back, full of snow, and the whole world was so white that he couldn't see beyond the wipers on his windscreen. The van started sliding about all over the place, and your dad said we'd never make it to the hospital.

So we gave up trying there and then, and you were born in a lay-by, in a blizzard, on an empty mountain pass road with not another soul in sight for miles. Your dad acted as midwife and made a brilliant job of it. It's amazing what that man can do when he stops grumbling and gets on with it.

After the blizzard was all over, he wrapped you in a blanket and lifted you to the van window to see the world into which you'd been born. The mountains and valleys stood like white ghosts beneath an early-morning sky, but the river had long-gone as well, and all that remained of that unforgettable night was a pale moon growing paler by the moment as the sun broke over the mountains, setting the snowy landscape on fire.

It was a wonderful sight. So wonderful that your dad opened the van door and carried you out into it. But, instead of being impressed, you started howling. He thought it was the cold air, and rushed you back inside. But I knew you were crying because you'd come too late. It was as if the snowy landscape was the support band, and the silver river in the sky the main attraction, come to earth for a once-in-a-lifetime performance, and you had missed it and you knew.

You howled as if you'd never stop. Howled the way that mad dogs do at the moon. If you ever hear them out in the wilds, on a lonely night with not a soul around, you'll know how chilling they can be. But, if a newborn baby's doing it, to show that it's alive, it's awe-inspiring. Believe me.

And that's the way you got your name. MAD DOG MOONLIGHT. It's not some crazy name we came up with off the top of our heads. It's the name you earned for yourself the day that you were born. It's your name, and don't you ever let anybody take it from you, because it's who you are.

Part I
The Gap

1

Ryan Lewis

When Mad Dog arrived, one of the first things Aunty did was give him a new name. He tried explaining that he had one, thanks, and didn't need another, but she insisted that he couldn't go round being called after some dog.

Mad Dog couldn't see why not. He sat on the edge of an enormous armchair in an unknown sitting room in a house he'd never seen before while an aunty – who was as unknown as everything else – told him that people would make fun of him if he went round telling them he was called Mad Dog Moonlight.

'All right, I won't say anything,' Mad Dog said, as if the problem was easy to solve. 'If they ask my name, I'll say I don't know.'

'You've *got* to have a name,' the aunty insisted. 'Everybody has a name. People need to know what to call you. What's your real name? You know, the name on your birth certificate – surely you know that?'

Mad Dog didn't know what a birth certificate was any more than what this unknown aunty meant when she talked about real names. But he knew he wasn't Ryan, which was what she decided to call him. Ryan with a Lewis at the end of it, chosen because it was her husband's family name and, if it did for them, it could do for him.

It wasn't exactly the best of starts. Until now, Mad Dog Moonlight had always felt invincible and brave, wolfish and wild, a free boy of the open road with not a care in the world. But with a name like Ryan Lewis he felt like someone's pet, waiting for his owners to come and collect him.

The trouble, though, was that they didn't. That first day Mad Dog refused to eat or talk or get off the big chair, but simply looked out of the window waiting for his parents. By bedtime they hadn't come for him and the new-found aunty led him upstairs to a bedroom that she said was 'his'. It had a cot in one corner, for his baby brother, a bed for him and lots of toys and picture books that she referred to as 'yours while you're here, so feel free to enjoy them'.

Mad Dog couldn't work out what was going on. The bedroom was bigger than his parents' entire van, and he felt lost in it. He lay awake half the night, listening out for them. But by morning they hadn't come and, by the following night, they still hadn't come. And, by the end of the first week, there was *still* no sign of them.

Other children passed through the aunty's house, and they had parents who dropped them off and came back later. But no parents came for Mad Dog, and sometimes he'd tear around the house, yelling in the other children's faces or throwing things at the aunty and, at other times, he'd sit in the big chair, refusing to talk or eat, simply saying over and over again, 'I want to go home.'

Mad Dog hated this strange house. It didn't shake like his parents' van, but always stayed solid and in exactly the same place. Its walls didn't rattle as if they were alive. Its floors didn't roll with the motion of the road. Its windows always opened out on the same view.

Aunty said that Mad Dog was to look upon it as his home. 'No. 3, The Gap, Aberystwyth Harbour,' she said. 'From now on, if anybody asks, it's your address.'

But *why* was it his address? What had happened to his real home? One day he'd been his old, usual self, living his old, usual life with his mother and his dad and, the next, he'd been turned into someone called Ryan Lewis who lived with an uncle and aunty he'd never met before and a stream of children, who came and went, who he didn't know and didn't want to.

Aunty tried coaxing him to make friends but Mad Dog wouldn't have it. What did he want friends for? All he wanted was his old life. And how could he make friends, anyway, with weird children like these who watched telly all the time and played with stupid toys, and never did any of the sorts of things he was used to doing, like building dams in streams, climbing trees and being taught by his dad to catch fish with his bare hands?

So Mad Dog ignored these other children when they came round, and took to spending most of his time upstairs at his bedroom window. He refused all Aunty's attempts at mothering him, and the only person that he relaxed around was his baby brother, whom he'd jig up and down on his lap, promising that their parents would soon come for them.

Mad Dog's brother's name was Elvis – which was another thing that had set Aunty off when they'd first arrived. 'Elvis Preseli,' he'd said when Aunty asked. And she'd replied, 'You must be joking!'

But Mad Dog wasn't joking. Why would he do that? He tried explaining to Aunty about Elvis being

11

named after a local saint who came from the Preseli Mountains in west Wales, where he'd been born. But Aunty insisted that the name Elvis was out. Again she said that people would laugh. She didn't explain what was so funny but, after that, Mad Dog's brother became Eric Lewis, just as he was Ryan Lewis.

Mad Dog didn't want them to be Lewises, but he had no choice. Everybody in Aberystwyth, or so it seemed to him, was a Lewis. The family was everywhere. Right across that area of the harbour set behind the River Rheidol and known as 'the Gap', aunties, uncles, cousins, nieces, nephews, grandparents and grandchildren filled almost every house. Half the children who came to play were Lewises, and the other half were Williamses from Aunty's side of the family. But most of the Williamses turned out to be married to Lewises anyway, so there wasn't much to choose between them.

Not that it made any difference to Mad Dog. Williamses and Lewises counted for nothing as far as he was concerned. All that counted was the family he'd left behind, not the one that he was stuck with now. Aunty could go on for as long as she liked about him being 'one of us', but she and Uncle could have been anybody as far as he was concerned – not just Lewises or Williamses, but witches, robbers, big bad wolves. *Or even school teachers.*

In the old life that he'd left behind, Mad Dog had heard talk of a terrible place called *school* where his parents seemed to think he might end up if they weren't careful. Mad Dog didn't know what school was – only that it had apparently never done them any good and was best avoided.

For the first few days after arriving at No. 3, he lay awake at night, worrying that this house was school, and that Aunty and Uncle had kidnapped him and were going to do terrible things to him. Uncle was a brawny ex-seaman, six foot three in his socks, with muscles the size of hams and a head built like a battering ram. And Aunty might be short and skinny, but she didn't look any less tough.

In the end, with still no parents coming to his rescue, Mad Dog decided that the best thing was to go and find them. He went at night when he thought everyone was asleep. Dressing quietly so as not to wake his brother, he crept downstairs, opened the front door and headed off into the night. He didn't have a clue where he was going but, at the end of the Gap, where the River Rheidol ran under the road bridge before flowing out into the harbour, it came to him that the world was a big place and perhaps he should wait until he'd grown up a bit.

Mad Dog was on the way back to No. 3, trying to work out which was the right house because they all looked much the same to him, when he bumped into Uncle coming after him. Uncle didn't shout or anything like that, but it was obvious that he was rattled at having to come out in the middle of the night. When they got back indoors, Aunty was obviously rattled too – though she did manage a quick hug before telling Mad Dog off.

Even Elvis seemed to have caught the mood of general rattlement, looking up from his cot with an accusing face, as if he knew that Mad Dog had walked out on him. Mad Dog only had to look at him to feel ashamed.

After that, he tried to be a better brother and stop thinking about running away. Instead of burying himself in deep, dark thoughts, he tried to lighten up for Elvis, playing with him, helping at feeding time, rocking him when he had wind and even changing the odd nappy. Then at night-time in their room together, he lulled his brother to sleep with their parents' stories. He told their dad's favourite one about them having Trojan blood and being twice as brave as anybody else, his mother's favourite one about the silver river, and a string of others about doing what she'd always called 'trusting in the power of the open road'.

'*You'll always be rovers,*' their mother had said. '*One only has to look at you to see you've got travelling blood. You're dark like a pair of secrets – dark like the earth itself. Fierce, and flint-hard, and you'll always end up on the move. It's your curse and calling, just like it's mine. You'll never settle down.*'

Well, she was wrong about that one! Some nights, after he'd talked Elvis to sleep, Mad Dog would cry into his pillow. He refused to do it in front of Aunty because of what his dad had said about being brave. But the darkness was different. Here, if he dishonoured his Trojan blood, no one needed to know.

But one night Aunty heard Mad Dog. 'What's the matter?' she said, coming into his room and sitting on his bed. 'You can tell me. Come on, Ryan. There are lots of things that we could talk about if you'd only open up. You know you can tell your aunty anything. There's a good boy.'

Mad Dog turned away from her. There were things

he might have opened up about – mysteries in his life that he couldn't explain – but how could he talk about them to someone who wouldn't even call him by his proper name?

'Ryan, *speak to me*,' Aunty said. 'You've been silent ever since you've got here, and this can't go on. You've got a story to tell and we want to know what it is. We want to help you, but we can't if you won't tell us anything about yourself. Is there something you're frightened of? Something that happened to you that you want to forget? Do you have a secret? Come on, Ryan, open up.'

Still Mad Dog didn't answer, and Aunty finally gave up, saying that, if he changed his mind, he knew where she was.

'What was wrong?' he heard Uncle saying as she climbed back into bed.

'He wouldn't tell me,' she answered.

'He's a strange one,' Uncle said.

'You'd be strange if the police had found you wandering around with a baby in your arms and you didn't know whose it was, or who you were or where you'd come from,' Aunty said.

She made excuses for Mad Dog all the time. Of all the children who came through the house, he was the special one. When he wouldn't eat, she refused to scold. When he threw a mad dog fit and started chucking things about, she tried to laugh it off. Even when he stood for days on end staring out of the window, his face as blank as a plain piece of paper, she refused to let it get to her.

Those were the worst times, though. And not just worst for Aunty, who couldn't get through to Mad

Dog or understand what was going on inside his head, but worst for him too, who felt as if a bottomless pit lay inside of him and he was falling down it. There'd be times when his refusal to eat would go on for days, and nameless terrors inside of him seemed to rise to the surface, almost close enough to touch.

Sometimes Mad Dog would feel so frightened about what was happening to him that he'd wet himself or do even worse. Then Aunty's sisters would see the extra washing hanging on the line and huddle in the kitchen with her, saying that though she'd had years of fostering experience behind her and been on courses run by social services and things like that, perhaps this time she'd bitten off more than she could chew.

Mad Dog heard them, but he didn't understand what they were on about. Words like 'fostering' meant nothing to him. One day somebody called 'his social worker' came round to talk to him, but he didn't know what a social worker was and nobody explained.

She was a tall woman with a wobbly face who encouraged Mad Dog to draw pictures of his old life. Could he draw his parents? she wanted to know. Could he draw his home? Was it on a street? In a town, or in a village? Did it stand alone? Could he remember anything in particular about it? A colour on the front door? A number? A pet? A garden? Any sort of landmarks anywhere nearby?

Mad Dog must have a home somewhere, the social worker insisted. Was it in the Preseli Mountains like Aunty had suggested, or somewhere inland among the mountains of mid-Wales? Or did Mad Dog belong further away than that, over the border in England, maybe in a city somewhere, far from where he'd been

16

found? The police had looked everywhere, but they'd drawn a blank. Surely there was some place waiting for him to come back. And if not a mother or father, then grandparents, aunties, uncles. *Somebody*.

But Mad Dog wouldn't answer. When people asked him questions like this, a deep silence would fall upon him and it wasn't just a matter of being unable to remember things – he didn't even *want* to remember them. Didn't people understand that memories were dangerous things, best left untouched? If things were slipping from his grasp – like his parents' faces, for example – perhaps it was all that he deserved.

Mad Dog didn't want to lose the memory of his parents' faces, but the fear rose up in him that perhaps he'd done something terrible and they were angry with him. He'd better behave at No. 3, he told himself, or else it just might happen here as well. He'd try harder to be the Ryan Lewis that everybody wanted, smiling back when people smiled at him and asked how he was today, and eating what they gave him and being a good boy.

But, for all his trying, the old Mad Dog Moonlight was never far behind. At the slightest provocation, Aunty and Uncle would find themselves confronted by an angry child, more wolf than boy, snarling, biting and throwing things about.

Then the social worker would be invited round again, and Aunty's sisters would chip in with their good advice. 'Syndromes' and 'psychological assessments' would be talked about, but Aunty wouldn't have any of it. Against all comers, she stood her ground.

'We're in unknown territory,' she kept on saying. 'We can't play this by the book. How often have any of us come across a child who doesn't know where he's come from, let alone who he is? I mean, when he first arrived, he thought he was a dog and his brother was Elvis Presley! There's a story in that boy waiting to come out. And one day it will, you mark my words, and I'll be there for him when it does. He hasn't got a syndrome and he doesn't need assessments. All he needs is time, and a bit of love.'

2
The Ffon

One morning Mad Dog awoke to find a walking cane lying across the bottom of his bed. It was a tall, thin thing, made of polished wood, with a silver topknot. Mad Dog was certain it hadn't been there when he'd gone to sleep the night before, and yet there was something strangely familiar about it.

Mad Dog only had to pick it up, feel its weight in his hand and run his fingers over the topknot for something from his old life to come flooding back. He could see his mother again, see the face he'd almost forgotten, lost in rapt attention as she engraved a pattern on the topknot with the little tool she used for making silver jewellery. Then suddenly he could see his dad too – see him polishing the whole finished cane from top to toe, and hear him saying that it was his, Mad Dog's.

'It's your *ffon*,' he said, using the Welsh word for walking cane, which Mad Dog thought he had forgotten. 'We've made it especially for you. It's for when you grow up and want to know who you are. It's not a toy – so don't you play around with it. Over my dead body, after all the trouble we've taken, are you going out with it and losing it somewhere!'

Mad Dog dropped the *ffon* immediately when he remembered that. Was that what he'd done? Taken it somewhere and lost it, and lost himself into the bargain?

Aunty called upstairs that breakfast was ready. Mad

Dog thought about hiding the *ffon* under the bed. But curiosity got the better of him and he took it downstairs instead, hoping that Aunty could explain where it had come from.

'At last,' she said as he walked through the door. 'What does it take to make you get up in the morning? What time do you call this?'

Mad Dog sat down with the *ffon*. Aunty put his breakfast in front of him. He tapped the *ffon* on the floor, but she didn't say anything except, 'Well, aren't you going to eat?'

Mad Dog tapped the *ffon* on the floor again, only louder. Why was Aunty ignoring it? And what did she know that she wasn't telling him? When she'd tucked him up in bed last night, there'd been no *ffon*. When she'd turned out the lights, there'd been no *ffon*. When he'd gone to sleep there'd been no *ffon*, and now here was his *ffon* and surely she, of all people – here in her own house – had to know what was going on!

'Stop teasing me,' he said. 'Where did this come from? You must know. Did someone drop it off? And did they leave me a message?'

Aunty looked confused. 'I don't know what you're on about,' she said. 'Nobody dropped anything off, certainly not that stick. You had it with you when you came.'

Anger rose inside Mad Dog. He banged the *ffon* on the floor, knowing that he hadn't brought it with him, no way. But was it possible that his parents had brought it? Were they here somewhere, waiting to leap out, crying, 'Surprise, surprise'?

Mad Dog leapt down from the table, sent his

breakfast flying and started tearing round the house, searching everywhere for his parents. Aunty came after him, crying at him to calm down, but he started swinging the *ffon* at her, sending ornaments flying.

'Dear God, Ryan!' Aunty cried. 'What's up with you? Give me that stick!'

'It's not a stick – it's a *ffon*!' yelled Mad Dog.

'I don't care what it is!' Aunty yelled back.

She grabbed Mad Dog and tried to wrench the *ffon* out of his grasp. For a moment there was a tussle, but he was just a little boy and she was a strong woman, and it didn't take much for her to get the *ffon* and kick it out of the way. Mad Dog tried to get it back, but Aunty held him off.

'I want my mother!' he screamed into her face. 'I want my dad! I want to go home! *Get out of my way, you stupid old cow!*'

Aunty flinched at that. Her cheeks burned red and she held on to Mad Dog until he'd calmed down. Then she gave him such a telling-off that he was certain she'd phone the police and get them to take him away.

Mad Dog tried to say sorry, but couldn't help following it up with, 'Give me back my *ffon*.'

In the end Aunty relented and gave it to him. 'I promise you that no one brought it here,' she said. 'You had it with you when you came.'

'I didn't have *anything*,' Mad Dog said.

Aunty shrugged. 'Suit yourself,' she said, 'but, the way I saw it, you had your brother and you had this stick.'

Mad Dog spent the rest of the day trying to work it all out. He'd absolutely no memory of arriving with the cane. But then, if he thought about it, he'd precious little memory of anything else about that day, apart from a journey in a police car and then standing on the doorstep with a policewoman by his side holding Elvis in her arms.

He could have brought the *ffon* with him, like Aunty said. But his dad's words *over my dead body* kept ringing in his head. And what if his dad was dead? Ever since arriving at No. 3, Mad Dog had been waiting for his parents to come and get him. But what if they didn't? What if the *ffon* was all he had left?

Mad Dog put the walking cane in the back of the wardrobe in his bedroom, where he wouldn't have to look at it all the time, or feel his past every time he touched it or imagine his parents stooping over it. Better that way, he told himself. Better let them go. Better shut them up. Better close the door on them. Better lock the door, and lose the key and forget the streams he'd played in once, the roads he'd travelled on, the place names, family names, and everything else.

Better be the boy that Aunty wanted, or else she just might send him away.

And then where would he go?

3

The Mermaid on the Beach

Mad Dog calmed down after that. Aunty told herself that he was settling in, but perhaps she knew in her heart that he wasn't really because, when the social worker started talking about school, she insisted on keeping him at home. No one knew how old he was, she said, and he certainly wasn't as ready for school as Little Luke next door – her sister's son who'd recently started in Mrs Heligan's class.

So Mad Dog stayed at home, playing in the garden or on the barge den stuck on the grass at the top of the Gap. He loved the barge den from the first time he ever climbed on board. Even with old scraps of moth-eaten carpet and crates for chairs and tables, it felt far more like home than No. 3. He loved the way the barge den rattled when he ran about on it. It almost made him feel as if he was on the open road. Even having to share it with the other Gap children was bearable. But, when he had it to himself and could sit watching the sun on the Rheidol as it flowed through the harbour, he was at his happiest.

The harbour felt new, with its yachts and pontoons and modern flats on St David's Quay, but the Rheidol felt old. It came from somewhere in the past, and it was on a journey. Mad Dog would rock for hours in the hammock that Uncle had strung up for him, watching it flowing past and wondering where its journey took it after it reached the sea.

Sometimes he'd even dream about it, falling asleep in the hammock, lulled by its gentle swaying motion. Back in his bedroom at No. 3, his dreams were often dark and heavy and he'd wake up in a panic. There'd be flames in them, and falling shadows and the sound of howling out there in the night.

But the dreams Mad Dog had on the barge den were sunshine dreams, full of light and colour. He'd awaken feeling good. There were rivers in his dreams, and breaking blue waves on golden shorelines. One day there was even a mermaid and the dream was so real that Mad Dog was sure it had once happened.

In the dream, Mad Dog was on a great expanse of beach with a shelf of sand dunes running across the top of it and his parents' van parked against them, half-buried in long grass. It wasn't one of those nice, clean beaches that holidaymakers like to sunbathe on, but strewn with pebbles, rock pools and slippery seaweed. Even so, Mad Dog played for hours, trawling through the pools and making towers of shells and stones.

Finally it got dark and a little wind came up from the ocean and blew into the bay, sending rows of white-topped waves running up the shingle. Mad Dog's mother called from the van that food was on the table and, on any other occasion, he'd have gone tearing home to eat.

But, on this occasion, he didn't go anywhere because his attention was caught by – a mermaid.

Mad Dog had never seen a mermaid before, but he had no doubt what he was looking at. He was his mother's son after all, and had heard her stories. He knew that there were elves living in the mountains, tree spirits in the forests and mermaids in Cardigan Bay where their secret kingdom lay beneath deep waters.

But Mad Dog had never thought to see a mermaid in the flesh. And one thing was certain about that mermaid – she was definitely in the flesh! Her shoulders were bare, her breasts were pink, her fishy mermaid's tail was as shiny as a piece of living seaweed, her hair was wet and golden and she had the brightest eyes Mad Dog had ever seen.

He stopped and stared in amazement, and the mermaid stared back at him, fearlessly meeting his gaze. Out on the horizon, a ship winked. Off around the headland, a lighthouse blinked its steady pulse. Somewhere among the sand dunes, Mad Dog's mother called again. But none of them were as real as the mermaid in front of him, her look steady and amused as if to say, 'Well, little boy, what do you think?'

Mad Dog would have answered, if he could only think what to say. Instead he found himself dashing up the shingle, yelling, 'You've got to see this! Come on! Quickly!! *Come and see!! THERE'S A MERMAID ON THE BEACH!!*'

By the time Mad Dog returned, however, the mermaid had gone. 'Where is she, then?' his dad had said, running up and down the shoreline as if he thought the whole thing was a joke.

But Mad Dog's mother didn't think it was a joke. She stood before the ocean with eyes as black as pearls, savouring how rare and wonderful the world could be. Mad Dog watched her, fascinated by her expression. And, later on the barge den, awakening from dreaming, he could still see that expression, and it was so real in his mind that he knew it was a memory and not just a dream.

After that Mad Dog couldn't stop thinking about mermaids. They could be out there, he kept telling himself, even now, waiting to surprise him, bringing back an old life when his parents hadn't been angry with him and hadn't been dead, and weren't just a distant dream, but were still real.

In the end, unable to stop thinking about what he'd lost and just might be able to find again, Mad Dog took himself off on a mermaid hunt. He did it one night when everyone else was asleep, reckoning that mermaids could be out there somewhere on the seashore, even as he lay there in his bed.

It was a thrilling prospect imagining them bathing in calm waters in the shallows of the beach or combing out their hair in the shadows under the pier. Mad Dog got up, dressed quietly so as not to wake Elvis, and set off, telling himself that they could be *anywhere*.

The front door was unlocked, as were all the doors along the Gap, and easy to open. Mad Dog crossed the road outside No. 3 and went to look over the harbour wall. When he didn't see anything, he went along to the end of the Gap and looked at the River Rheidol as it cut a path through the harbour. It winked at him in the darkness, as black as ebony, with the coloured harbour lights reflected in it.

There were no mermaids to be seen, so Mad Dog turned his back on the harbour and set off for the seafront. Aunty and Uncle would be furious if they found out what he was up to. But, promising to be back before they awoke, he climbed down the first set of steps he came to and started walking along the beach.

All the way, Mad Dog's eyes were fixed on the shoreline. But, by the time he reached the pier, he hadn't seen a single mermaid. Not that he allowed that to put him off. Hoping for more luck under the pier, Mad Dog crept into its shadows, telling himself that the mermaids around Aberystwyth were probably less bold than the ones you found on lonely beaches where there weren't so many people to look at them.

He picked his way between the massive girders holding up the pier, tripping over empty beer cans and broken wine bottles. Eventually, he found somewhere to sit that gave him the widest possible view yet enabled him to remain hidden. Here he curled up against the chill of the night, reckoning he had at least an hour of uninterrupted mermaid-spotting ahead of him before he'd have to return home.

It was here that Uncle found him hours later, fast asleep. Night had turned to day, bringing with it clouds and driving rain. Mad Dog awoke to find himself so cold that he could scarcely move. He'd no idea how Uncle had known where to look for him but was glad to be discovered.

They walked home together, awkward and uncomfortable. Mad Dog had no answer to Uncle's question, 'What have you got to say for yourself?' How could he even begin to explain? Maybe things like mermaids had happened in his old life, but here on this grey winter's morning in Aberystwyth, no one would believe how fabulous and extraordinary the world could be.

4
School

When Aunty discovered that Mad Dog had spent the night under the pier where the drunks hung out, she was angrier than the first time he'd run away.

'Ryan, *Ryan* – there of all places!' she cried out. 'All sorts of things go on under the pier! You never know who you'll find there. Anything could happen in the darkness where nobody can see. A little boy like you, out on your own. It doesn't bear thinking about! And what were you doing anyway, running off like that?'

Mad Dog tried explaining that he hadn't been running off. But Aunty wouldn't let him get a word in edgeways. 'That's the second time you've done it,' she said, scarcely pausing for breath, 'and it's got to be the last. The world's not safe for a child out on his own. There are some dangerous people around – and I'm not just talking about the pier. You mustn't ever go near strangers, or answer if they speak to you, or even look at people you don't know, not if you can help it. *Do you understand what I'm saying?*'

Mad Dog reckoned that he did, but it never occurred to him that he'd have to put Aunty's warning into practice quite so soon. A couple of days after the mermaid hunt, he awoke to find long grey trousers made of itchy material waiting for him at the end of his bed, along with a grey sweater that was too big for him and a brand new, horribly white-looking shirt.

'What are these for?' he said.

'You're off to school,' Aunty said.

Mad Dog's first thought was that he was being punished for running away. But it was a funny sort of punishment, he reckoned when he got there, because the place was full of exactly the sort of strangers that Aunty had warned him about. In fact, Mad Dog had never met so many strangers all together in one place in his life. Remembering Aunty's words of warning, he refused to go too close to them, answer if they spoke or even look at them if he could help it.

Little Luke was in his class, but that didn't make Mad Dog feel any better. So were some of the other children who came to play on the barge den or were dropped off by their mothers at Aunty's house. Her nephew Hippie – a friendly, gangling boy whose mother did yoga and had crystals hanging at her windows in long strings – was one of them, and another nephew Rhys – whose father was a footballer and trained the family 'team' – was another.

Mad Dog knew them both but wouldn't play with them, eat lunch with them, share books or paints with them, or even speak to them if he could help it. And he was especially careful not to have anything to do with the stranger in charge of them all, who said she was his teacher.

Aunty would have been proud of him, Mad Dog reckoned. From the moment he encountered Mrs Heligan in registration, he reckoned her to be the most dangerous stranger of all.

'Good morning, Mrs Heligan,' all the other children said when she called out their names. But when she called out *Ryan Lewis*, remembering what Aunty had told him, Mad Dog wouldn't say a thing. He wouldn't even look at Mrs Heligan and, when she tried to come near him, he backed away.

Mad Dog kept it up all day too. Instead of lining up for assembly, sitting where Mrs Heligan put him, going out to play when she told him to, answering when she asked him things, or doing anything else that she expected of him, Mad Dog sat staring into space.

When Aunty came to pick him up, Mrs Heligan put it to her loudly enough for all the other mothers to hear that Mad Dog should have started school weeks ago.

'I don't know whose decision it was to keep the poor child at home,' she said, looking pointedly at Aunty, 'but it was a terrible mistake. He's going to need some serious sorting out if he's ever to become a social animal. And it isn't going to happen overnight.'

Mad Dog blushed. He wasn't sure what a 'social animal' was, and was even less sure he wanted to become one. But Aunty's blush was of a different nature. It wasn't often that people dared to call her considered decisions for the welfare of others *terrible mistakes*. All the way home she was in a foul mood and Mad Dog thought that, despite his best efforts, he'd let her down. Only later, over tea at home with Luke's mum, did he realise that it wasn't him Aunty was cross with, but Mrs Heligan herself.

'She's a stupid woman,' Aunty said. 'She doesn't have a clue how to handle children properly. I never would have let her get her hands on Ryan if I'd had any choice. You know, she only got that job because she's the head teacher's niece. I mean, why else would they have chosen her? She doesn't have a brain in her head.'

Mad Dog didn't care whose niece Mrs Heligan was – all he cared about was that he'd taken his punishment like a man and could now get on with the rest of his life. Expecting everything to return to normal, he was astonished next morning to wake up and find a clean shirt waiting for him at the end of the bed, along with the same old uniform.

'What's that for?' he said, eyeing it all with suspicion.

'For school, of course,' Aunty said.

'You mean I've got *today* as well?' Mad Dog said.

'But of course you have. Just like everybody else.'

'But haven't I been punished enough?'

'Punished for what? School's not a punishment. Whatever are you on about?'

Mad Dog tried to grasp what Aunty was saying. If school wasn't a punishment, he didn't know what it was. 'Have I got to go tomorrow too?' he said.

'And the next day and the next,' said Aunty.

'You mean, I've got to go to school *for ever*?'

'Not for ever – just until you're grown up,' Aunty said.

In a state of shock, Mad Dog was finally persuaded to get dressed. Uncle was sorry for him but Aunty said she couldn't see what the fuss was all about.

'If you give school a chance, it'll be the best time of your life,' she said. 'I loved it myself and made loads of friends. Just you wait and see. Once you get used to it, you'll be glad you went.'

Mad Dog wondered how long it would take for that to happen. He certainly didn't feel glad now and, when Aunty delivered him directly into the hands of Mrs Heligan, he didn't feel glad then either. Again the day began with registration. This time, when Mrs Heligan called out, 'Good morning, Ryan', Mad Dog muttered, 'Yes.'

But this wasn't good enough for Mrs Heligan. 'Ah, I see we're speaking today,' she said, fixing Mad Dog with her cold blue eyes. 'Keep it up, boy. At least we're getting somewhere. But *good morning, Mrs Heligan* – that's what I want.'

Mad Dog muttered the required words, but swore to hate Mrs Heligan for ever. He'd tried to please her and she hadn't even noticed. For the rest of the day, he steadfastly refused to meet her eye or say another word, reckoning that, no matter how nice she was to special favourites like the class princess, Grendel Griffiths, she was still one of those dangerous strangers that Aunty had warned him about.

This set a pattern for the weeks to come. Despite all Mrs Heligan's efforts to 'sort out' Mad Dog, he still doggedly refused to cooperate. What was the point of doing otherwise? Mrs Heligan plainly had him down as a troublemaker whatever he did, always blaming him when things went wrong.

Even when a gang of hulking top class boys ganged up on him in the playground, she insisted he was the one who'd started it all. Little Luke tried explaining what had really happened, because she hadn't been there to see. So did Hippie and Rhys, who had seen everything from the start. But the big boys got off, and Mrs Heligan insisted on punishing Mad Dog by taking away his book corner privileges. As if he wanted to look at stupid books, anyway, or do anything other than tear them up!

In the end, a conference was called to decide what

to do with such a difficult child. Aunty and Uncle attended, and so did Mad Dog's social worker, who was certain that he had a syndrome – something that Mrs Heligan latched on to immediately, suggesting that what he needed was a 'key worker'.

Everybody seemed to like the idea, except for Aunty, who reckoned that this would only make Ryan stick out more than he already did. 'There's nothing wrong with him that time won't sort out,' she said. 'I keep saying this, but no one will listen. He'll be all right as long as we all do our jobs. And I mean *all* of us. It's no good Mrs Heligan here passing the buck. She's got to make this work as much as anybody else.'

Mrs Heligan flushed and said she'd never passed the buck in her life. She glared at Aunty as if she was one of those difficult parents who made teaching such a burden. Aunty smiled back at her, but she wasn't smiling later, back at home when she sat Mad Dog down and gave it to him straight.

'You've got to pull yourself together,' she said. 'There's a limit to how much I can stick up for you. Stop messing around, or God alone knows where this will end up. They've had enough, Ryan, believe me. That Mrs Heligan has it in her to make your life a misery.'

Mad Dog tried after that. The last thing he wanted was for his life to be any more of a misery than it already was. He still didn't speak to Mrs Heligan unless he had to, but he tried harder to join in and act the same as everybody else. And it must have worked too, because Mrs Heligan told the head teacher that she'd 'cracked the boy'.

But beneath these small improvements in Mad

Dog's behaviour, anyone with half a sense could see that things weren't right. A strange remoteness settled upon Mad Dog, and the more he tried to fit in the worse it became. Every day he was surrounded by people, and yet terrible deep silences would fall upon him and he'd feel more and more alone. Sometimes he'd have dreams too – faceless dreams without shape but full of dread. The people around him didn't know about his dreams and they didn't know about the boy he really was.

And, as time went by, he felt as if he didn't even know himself.

Day after day, he'd trail home from school, eat his tea, watch a bit of telly, play with his baby brother and go to bed. He smiled when people wanted him to, said yes instead of no and reckoned he'd fooled everyone that things were fine.

But Aunty wasn't fooled. As time went by, she could sense Mad Dog going further and further into himself. There were things she couldn't get at – things that were slipping out of reach – and she didn't like it. She didn't like it one bit.

One evening she sat Mad Dog down and tried to get him talking. Unfortunately for her though, it had been a bad day in school for Mad Dog and the last thing he wanted was to talk. She started off by asking what he liked doing best in class, who his friends were and if anything in particular was troubling him. But he refused to answer any of her questions and went up to his room.

Aunty followed, asking if there was anything he'd like to talk about, and Mad Dog went downstairs again and sat in front of the telly. She turned off the telly, saying she couldn't take much more of his deep silences, and he went looking for Elvis. She took Elvis off him and he went and hid in the wardrobe in his bedroom, pulling the door behind him and praying for the whole wide world to *go away*.

It was here, alone at last, that Mad Dog came across his *ffon*. For ages now he'd forgotten all about it, but suddenly it was in his hands again.

Mad Dog looked down at the silver topknot. It couldn't have chosen a better moment to come back into his life. Slowly he started talking to it. He couldn't talk to Aunty but, as if it was the most natural thing in the world, he found himself talking to a walking cane.

In the end Mad Dog told it everything too. There was nothing, he discovered, that he couldn't say. His *ffon* wasn't cross when he said he hated school. It didn't tell him to try harder when he said he couldn't get the hang of reading. It didn't tell him that Mrs Heligan was a nice person really when he said he hated her. And it completely understood when he told it about the key worker whom Mrs Heligan had brought in today over Aunty's head, even though she'd insisted he didn't need one.

'I can't see what's so wrong with me,' Mad Dog said. 'No one else has got a key worker. Do they think I'm stupid or something?'

The *ffon* didn't answer, but that didn't bother Mad Dog. Every night after that, he climbed into the wardrobe and talked to his *ffon*, telling it whatever came into his head. Only when moods of deepest darkness came upon him did he remain silent. But then he'd hold his *ffon* anyway, and feel his mother's engraving beneath his fingers, and imagine her bowed over it again, and his father too, and draw comfort from it.

Over months the *ffon* came to know more about Mad Dog than any person. It knew exactly how he felt about living at No. 3 and what he liked and didn't like about Aunty and Uncle. It knew that Aunty's nephews, Luke, Hippie and Rhys were as near as he had to friends. It knew that Elvis was no longer a baby, as fast on his bottom as others were on two legs. It even knew that Mad Dog had become so used to being called Ryan that he hardly noticed any more.

In the end, Mad Dog didn't bother climbing into the wardrobe, but kept the walking cane close by where he could talk to it in comfort whilst lying in bed. Sometimes he nursed it in his arms, falling off to sleep like that.

And that was what he was doing one night when something about the *ffon* caught Mad Dog's attention. Maybe it was the moonlight that did it, shining through the window on to the silver topknot. But Mad Dog looked at the topknot and suddenly it came to him that it wasn't just decorated with a random pattern, but that the engraved shapes formed letters. Mad Dog turned on the light and looked at them more closely. For weeks his key worker had been trying to get him to read by recognising the shapes of individual letters. Now he ran his fingers over the topknot and knew for certain that what lay beneath them was a word. Letter by letter he traced it out, and he mightn't be able to read it but it still had to mean something!

That night Mad Dog lay awake for hours, staring at

his *ffon*, tingling with the certainty that it contained a secret message. He longed to understand what that message might be, but knew he couldn't ask for help because the letters were from his parents, and the message they contained was from them too, passed on to him like a sacred trust.

If he couldn't read them yet, there was only one thing for it.

He'd have to work at it until he could.

5

Swearing on the Book

After that, school had a purpose, and so did Mad
Dog. He was a boy with a secret and that made him as
good as, if not better than, anybody else. The
difference in him was plain to see. Even Mrs Heligan
noticed it, and so did Mad Dog's key worker. Still he
couldn't get the hang of half the things she tried to
teach him, but he did his best, he really worked.

And it wasn't just in school that a change was
evident, either. One Saturday morning – for no reason
that he could explain – Mad Dog joined the football
game being played on the grass at the top of the Gap.
No one invited him. He just turned up and got stuck
in.

He was good too. No one would have been as crazy
as to say hey, who did he think he was, barging in like
that? Aunty celebrated the team's victory with burgers
all round at the end of the game, and Mad Dog was
the hero of the hour. His passes had been brilliant for
someone who'd never played before, and he knew
how to score goals.

After that, Mad Dog was a fully signed-up member
of the family team and played so much football that
he even did it in his dreams. He started getting to
know who people were as well, who was related to
whom, where they all lived, who could be trusted and
who – like ghastly Grendel Griffiths and her gang of
adoring slaves – was best avoided at all costs.

Mad Dog was growing up, and his new-found friends were growing up too. Little Luke was growing so fast that nobody dared call him 'Little' any more – not unless they wanted to get their heads bashed in. When Luke's birthday came along, he suggested that he and Mad Dog celebrate together, seeing as Mad Dog didn't know when his real birthday was.

Luke's mum agreed, and so did Aunty, who decided to turn the day into one big party. The entire population of the Gap – or so it seemed to Mad Dog – crammed on board the barge den with presents, cards, streamers, poppers, funny hats and mountains of food. The barge den was decked out with ribbons and balloons, and had never looked so bright. Games were played with terrific prizes at the end, and two enormous sculptured cakes were brought out, each with candles on them. One was for Luke and shaped like a horse for no reason that anyone could explain, and the other – a massive chocolate cake – was for Mad Dog. It was a fantastic thing, shaped like a football boot, decorated with black, white and red icing and, when it was cut open, oozing with chocolate cream.

When Mad Dog went to bed that night, he couldn't remember ever having had more fun or eaten more food. Aunty and Uncle came in to say goodnight, wanting to know if he'd enjoyed himself. Mad Dog hugged them hard, then turned to go to sleep. But Aunty and Uncle had something else they wanted to say.

'We've had a great day too,' they said. 'Just like a proper family. In fact, after all this time we *are* a proper family, don't you think? It's nearly a year now since you came to stay, and that's long enough to want to put things on a legal footing. We couldn't love you more if you were our flesh and blood, and we couldn't love your brother more either, and we've no children of our own so what we are proposing is that we start proceedings to adopt you. That way, this could be your proper home, all signed and sealed and legal, and we could be your mum and dad. *What d'you think?*'

They beamed at him. Mad Dog tried to beam back, but inside he was stunned. It was impossible to put into words what he thought. No sooner had Aunty said those words 'mum and dad' than a spark of rage had flared up in him. How dared these people – no matter how long he'd lived with them or how many parties or presents they'd given him – think that they could ever be his parents?

'Of course you'll want to think it over,' Uncle said, recognising that a struggle was going on, but not understanding its true nature. 'We wouldn't want to rush you or anything like that.'

That night, Mad Dog ran away again. He did it properly this time, taking spare clothes, food and drink with him, and even the duvet off his bed. And he took his *ffon* as well. It was the first thing that he took, there in his hand without him even having to think about it, as if even the *ffon* knew that this wasn't his home and the time had come to get away.

Mad Dog held it tight, feeling its secret message beneath his palm, wondering what it meant and if it could be trusted to lead him home. He set off down the Gap, hoping for the best. His determination to find his parents, or at least unravel the mystery of what had happened to them, was renewed. He was determined too, to put as much distance as possible between himself and Aunty and Uncle. They were child-thieves. That's what they were. People who stole children from their parents, and Mad Dog had to get away from them even if he didn't know where he was going.

He followed the Rheidol, feeling safe because it was his river – the one he watched every day from his bedroom window, knowing everything on it from the swans under the bridge to the darting kingfishers and great swooping herons that glided over its surface looking for fish. It led him around the town, walking between roads and railway lines, offices, a retail development park and a big out-of-town supermarket. Eventually it brought him to the far side of Aberystwyth, where there were still houses around and street lights and cars, but a long silent road stretched off, into the night.

Mad Dog felt as if he'd walked for hours by now, and yet he hadn't even left Aberystwyth behind him yet. He shivered. Even with the duvet thrown over his shoulders, he couldn't help but feel cold.

I'm getting soft, he thought, remembering the old days when he'd played out in all weathers. Once a little bit of cold night wouldn't have bothered me. But then, that's what comes of being Ryan Lewis and not Mad Dog Moonlight.

It was a long time since Mad Dog had thought about his old name. Perhaps he could be that old self again. Be wolfish, wild and fearless. Perhaps that old person lay inside of him still, waiting to come out.

Telling himself that trying was better than not trying and going better than staying, Mad Dog pressed on. What was it his mother had always said about trusting in the power of the open road? Finally the last few houses fell behind him and nothing lay ahead but one single dark road. Mad Dog started down it. Every time a car swept past, he flung himself into the ditch in case it turned out to be Aunty and Uncle out looking for him. Soon he was covered in mud and soaking wet. Worse still, by now he'd lost the Rheidol.

Mad Dog clutched his *ffon*, determined not to lose that too.

Eventually, the lights of a village appeared somewhere on the road ahead, and he hurried towards it. At one end of the village, he found a cluster of allotments behind a tall fence. Climbing over the fence, he broke into the first shed he came to. Here he flung himself down among forks, spades, wheelbarrows, flower pots and sacks of potatoes, grateful for a place of shelter and trying to ignore how cold he was.

When day broke, Mad Dog was still awake, freezing cold and as stiff as a board. He was awake when Aunty opened her eyes on the new day and found him gone, but asleep by the time Uncle went out checking under the pier. He was still asleep when Uncle came back without him and phoned the police, and still asleep when Aunty phoned school and his social worker to let them know what was happening.

He slept on through the morning, and only when an old man in a quilted jerkin wanted to get to his wheelbarrow did he finally awake.

'Who are you?' the old man said, staring down at the small boy lying on his shed floor.

'I'm Mad Dog Moonlight,' Mad Dog said.

'And I'm Elvis Presley,' the old man said.

'No, that's my brother,' Mad Dog said.

The old man made Mad Dog a cup of tea on his camping stove, then tried again to get some sense out of him. Finally he gave up and, pretending to go for biscuits, phoned the police on his new fangled mobile. In no time at all Mad Dog found himself back at No. 3.

Here Aunty was beside herself with worry and Uncle as angry as a mountain in a thunderstorm. It wasn't so much the running away that did it, or even the timing of the thing, coming as it did straight after the party and his and Aunty's offer to give Mad Dog a proper home. It was the word *child-thief* that Mad Dog somehow managed to let slip. When he discovered what Mad Dog thought of him, Uncle's eyes flashed bolts of fury and words like *selfish*, *thoughtless* and *ungrateful* started hurtling about like thunderclaps.

'You should be ashamed of yourself! After all we've done for you! What we've been through, taking care of you! And all the good things we've tried to do for you! Well, if this is what you think of us, you can clear off somewhere else. We've had enough. Phone social services! Get your bloody social worker to sort you out! Or simply disappear – see if we care!'

He stomped off in a rage, slamming doors behind him. Aunty said he hadn't meant it. Her eyes were red with crying. Mad Dog only had to look at her to realise what a terrible thing he'd done. He hung his head and felt ashamed. He was a wicked boy. Aunty and Uncle had every reason to be upset. Of course they never, ever, would have tried to steal him. How could he possibly have thought otherwise? Whatever they'd meant when they'd talked about adopting him, it hadn't been that. People stole sweets and money and things like toys. They didn't steal children.

Finally Mad Dog went up to Aunty and tried to say sorry by standing next to her, wrapping his fingers round the soft material of her skirt and tugging it. She looked down at him.

'I don't mean to be bad,' he said. 'I don't like it like this. I want everything to be good, but it never is.'

Aunty smiled at that, and picked him up and hugged him. 'Oh, Ryan,' she said. 'What are we going to do with you?'

She must have given it some thought, because later she came in with the Lewis family Bible tucked under her arm – an enormous leather thing with covers falling off it and lists of names inside that went back for generations.

'Now then,' she said, setting it down before them both on the kitchen table. 'If you really mean it about wanting things to be good, this is what we're going to do. You're going to put your hand on this book – which is full of family history, and names and dates and people just like you and me, who probably wanted that as well – and you'll swear on your word of honour never to run away again. Then I'll swear never to talk to you about adoption again, not unless you invite me to, and that'll be the last we mention on the subject. You'll keep your word, so help you God, and so will I. And we'll start afresh. The both of us. We'll try to make a go of this. *What do you think?*'

6

The Storm

That same year, the worst storm in living memory hit Aberystwyth. It arrived one day without warning in a full-frontal attack. Nobody expected it, not even Mad Dog whose mother had once taught him how to read the colours of a storm before they hit. Without a single warning sign, it simply roared in.

Great white waves crashed between the stone pier and wooden jetty that marked the harbour's entrance, and the waters beyond them started seething. Pontoons smashed against each other and boats were crushed between them, their guy ropes flying about like whips, their prows smacking into each other like duelling swords.

A massive wind got up and the River Rheidol found itself forced back, its waves standing up in ridges like a dog's coat being stroked the wrong way. Usually the Rheidol was the king of the harbour, forcing everything out of its way as it flowed into the sea, but today the sea was king.

It came up over the grass where, until only half an hour ago, the boys had been playing football, lifted the barge den off the mud and threw it against the Gap wall. The boys tore home while they still could. The harbour in front of them was heaving like a washing machine full of sudsy water. Everywhere they looked, people were clinging to lamp posts and running for cover.

'Upstairs,' Aunty yelled when Mad Dog came hurrying up the path. 'Stay up there with Eric. I don't want either of you coming down. Unless I'm mistaken, we're in for a flood.'

Mad Dog wanted to help get ready for the flood, but Aunty wouldn't hear of it. 'I want to know you're safe,' she said. 'And I want to know your brother's safe as well. Do what I ask for once, and don't argue about it.'

She went out to the shed to collect the sandbags that were always kept down there for 'just in case'. Then Uncle came in from the harbour office, and he and Aunty piled them up against the front and back doors. They checked that all the downstairs windows were not only shut but bolted, put chairs on tables, took up rugs and electrical appliances and came upstairs to, as Uncle put it grimly, 'watch the fun'.

All along the Gap, Mad Dog could see the rest of the Lewis-Williams clan doing the same. They could have left their houses and headed inland, but they'd all decided to stay. They were harbour people, those Lewises and Williamses. Gap people. They'd seen storms before, and reckoned they could handle them.

But never a storm quite like this!

By now, a major battle was under way between the weather and the land – and the weather was winning hands down. It was only three o'clock in the afternoon, but the sky was black and the harbour had become as empty as midnight. Mad Dog watched the tide getting higher all the time, riding in on waves that looked as hard as iron. Right down the Gap, windows shook and roofs rattled. Even the brand new apartments on St David's Quay were shaken, slates blowing off their roofs and crashing on to the ground, and wheelie bins flying around, along with kiddies' bikes and skateboards.

Beyond the quay, the wind whipped its way round the bowl of the harbour in a low, furious hiss. Dinghies piled up against each other and even a couple of old iron fishing boats, weighing countless tons, strained their moorings and crashed against each other.

The storm raged for the rest of the day and on into the night. When Mad Dog went to bed it was still raging, and it was still going in the morning when he awoke. Uncle was out at the harbour office, where he'd spent the night helping coordinate rescue efforts, and, when he finally came in, he said that if any one was still out there at sea, they didn't stand a chance.

'I've never seen anything like it,' he said. 'It's as if the storm's a person. As if it's got a life all of its own and there's something in it, beyond the power of an ordinary storm. I don't know how else to explain it. It feels different to any other storm.'

The storm felt different to Mad Dog too. He sat up in his bedroom with Elvis, wrapped in duvets because the electricity was off, praying for it to blow itself out. Uncle had gone again, called back to the harbour office already because a new emergency had arisen. Mad Dog watched him fight his way back along the Gap. He was a big man, but he could hardly stand.

Behind him, Mad Dog saw waves roll in off the Atlantic like Neptune's cavalry charging the town's defences. Rain fell from the sky like sheets of deadly arrows and great white plumes of spray spewed everywhere like sea blood. Mad Dog thought of what

Uncle had said, and wondered if he was right. Did this storm really have a life all of its own?

Suddenly a small boat came limping into harbour through the gap between the wooden jetty and stone pier. Mad Dog stared at it in horrified fascination. The boat moved across his vision against a backdrop of seething waters and sheet rain. For a moment it disappeared, then against all hope Mad Dog saw it again – a ragged excuse of a boat, its mast at an angle, its sails in ribbons, keeling dangerously to one side.

Elvis stared as well. He pointed with his finger and said, '*Look, boat.*' But it took Aunty, standing behind them both, to draw in her breath and say, 'Oh, my God – there are *people* on that boat!'

The boat made it up the harbour, corkscrewing back and forth across the swollen waters of the Rheidol until it hovered directly opposite the entrance to the Gap. Here the wind picked it up and almost threw it into the Gap like an old toy being discarded. It crashed against the inner wall, right opposite No. 3. Elvis cried out and Mad Dog flinched and stepped back as if he thought the boat was going to end up flying through their window.

But, instead, it tipped over and started sinking. Mad Dog returned to the window just in time to see its mast disappearing behind the quay wall. Aunty saw it too, and leapt into action. She tore downstairs to phone for help and, when she couldn't get through, yelled, 'You stay here. Don't you dare move! I'm going over to the harbour office to get a rescue team!'

She staggered down the path – and the storm took her. Mad Dog watched it happening from his window. The wind lifted her clean off her feet and, if it hadn't been for Uncle coming the other way, she'd have ended up over the quay wall, along with the boat.

For a moment the two of them clung to each other. Mad Dog rattled on the window, calling them to come back. But, instead of turning for home, they started inching their way towards the quay. They were going to try and help the sailors, weren't they? Rain lashed against them and blasts of winds buffeted them. Elvis started crying. Mad Dog turned and snapped at him to shut up.

When he turned back, he couldn't see Aunty and Uncle any more. Long minutes passed, during which the rain got heavier and Elvis failed to shut up. Once Mad Dog caught a glimpse of what looked like Aunty lying flat on her belly, hanging over the edge of the wall. Another time he thought he saw Uncle with a massive coil of rope and something attached to the end of it. But then rain and clouds came down like pantomime curtains at the end of a show, and Mad Dog saw nothing until the rescue truck turned up, its yellow lights flashing on and off.

Then other bodies started moving about too, and Mad Dog caught another glimpse of Aunty, and then he saw Uncle and, between them both, he caught sight of a couple of bedraggled bodies wrapped up like turkeys in silver foil. The rescue team gathered round them. To begin with it looked as though they were going to be bundled into the truck and driven off. But then the truck raced off without them as if it had had another call, and Uncle, Aunty and the people they had rescued headed up the path to No. 3.

Mad Dog ran downstairs, flung open the front door and helped them in. Aunty said that the wind almost blew him away but all he remembered afterwards was the hall full of people all hugging each other with relief.

The boat people were exhausted, and shaking so much that Mad Dog wondered how they'd ever stop. They might look like hardened seafarers with their weather-beaten faces, but the storm had really done for them. Aunty went rushing about for blankets, towels and dry clothes. She made up spare beds as if a couple of new foster children had arrived in need of mothering. She poured tea down the sailors, forced them to eat against their will, then led them up to bed, where they fell asleep immediately.

Next morning, when they all awoke, the storm had gone. Mad Dog pulled back his curtains to find the sun shining down upon a harbour full of broken boats. The roof had come off the end of the harbour office. Windows were broken in the apartments on St David's Quay. Benches were upended, bins thrown about like litter – even a couple of cars had been turned upside down.

But the strangest thing of all was the eerie stillness. Apart from the Rheidol, still swollen to capacity as it rushed past the end of the Gap, nothing moved out there in the harbour. Not a person, car or even seagull, and definitely not a breath of wind. It was as if the harbour was holding its breath, not quite sure if the storm had really gone.

But it *had* gone. By the time that breakfast was over, the sound of hammering could be heard all over Aberystwyth. The sailors went to see what had become of their boat. The tide was out and they found it lying on its side in the mud. Uncle reckoned that it had had it, but they climbed on board anyway, to see what could be salvaged. The sea had got into every bit of it, but the sailors didn't seem disheartened. They'd be all right, they said. They'd recovered from worse.

They brought a massive metal trunk into the house and emptied out its contents. With it came a smell of sea salt that filled every room. Mad Dog watched as out came everything from cooking pans and sewing kits to balls of string, maps, shells, peacock feathers and an amazing quilt, embroidered with fairy stitches. Carved animals emerged, and wooden boxes inlaid with mother-of-pearl, tins of everything from dried beetles to green tea, leather pouches, silk scarves and a pure white tea-set made of porcelain so fine that Mad Dog could see through it when the woman sailor held it up.

Most of the saucers had been smashed but, for some reason, the cups were fine. In fact, most things in the trunk only needed washing to be put right. The sailors laid them out to dry, then returned to their boat where they spent the rest of the day seeing what could be salvaged. Late in the afternoon, exhausted by their efforts, they went back to bed. But, by suppertime, they were awake again and ready to tell the story of how the storm had hit them and how they'd survived.

After supper, Uncle built up the fire in the sitting room, and everybody crowded round. Mad Dog sat opposite the sailors and watched them intently. He was fascinated by them. Fascinated by the lines on their faces and their tough, calloused hands, which seemed to tell a story of their own.

The woman sailor was as tiny as a sunburnt elf and the man sailor looked like a proper swarthy seaman with his mop of hair tied back in a pigtail. His eyes were blue, but there was nothing soft about them. Like the woman's, they were flinty and determined and told of a hard life.

Aunty brought in mugs of hot chocolate all round. The sailors knocked theirs back in one go. They had a light way of inhabiting the room, sitting on the edge of their chairs as if ready to set off at a moment's notice. It was obvious that they weren't weekend sailors, and Mad Dog hung on to their every word. Perhaps the storm had gone, but something else had blown his way, something just as wild and strange.

Aunty asked where the sailors came from, and they shrugged and laughed and said nowhere in particular. Both talked at once, as tight together as a pair of barnacles on a hull. Their tales were tall but, they insisted, had all really happened. Whales, coral reefs, pirates, treasure islands, even mermaids – they'd seen them all.

'You mean you've really seen a mermaid?' Mad Dog said.

'Of course we have,' the man sailor said. 'And lots of other things as well. You wouldn't believe what's out there in the world.'

It was a long evening, but no one wanted it to end. For a few hours round the fire, they all knew what it was to be torn apart by hunger, beaten by the sun and bound by frost. They were all hung about with icicles, longing for a homeland and a journey's end.

'But there *is* no journey's end,' the woman sailor said. 'That's what we've discovered. All horizons lead to new ones, all discovery to even more.'

Mad Dog shivered. The woman sailor's words had a

magic about them that set him drifting off. When he returned to himself, he found Aunty clearing away cocoa mugs and talking about mundane things like going to bed. The evening was over. Mad Dog wanted more, but the sailors said there was always another day.

Everybody slept late next morning but, as soon as Mad Dog got up, he was on at the sailors to tell more stories. They promised they would later but, in the meantime, they had a boat to repair and Mad Dog and his family had a service to attend in the big town church.

This was a solemn occasion to commemorate the damage done by the storm and those who'd fought so valiantly to save lives. The entire town, it seemed, turned out and the church was full. The harbour master sat at the front, along with his team of volunteers, and the men and women from the rescue services and the mayor and mayoress. The vicar preached a sermon about surviving nature with the help of God, but Mad Dog wriggled all the way through it, his mind fixed on the sailors, wanting more of their stories, not this worthy sermon.

When they returned home, however, the sailors had gone. Mad Dog knew it the minute he stepped through the door. The smell of sea salt had gone too, and so had the metal trunk and all the things that had been drying out. All that remained were the porcelain cups, with a fifty-pound note tucked inside one of them, along with a letter written in fairy handwriting.

Aunty tried to read it, but the writing was so small that she even had a struggle wearing glasses.

'*You've been brilliant,*' she read at last. '*Thanks for*

everything. Boat repaired – at least as good as we can get it for now. Tide right. The sea calls. Sorry we don't have the time to say goodbye. We'll never forget your kindness to us. Please keep the cups. A little something to remember us by. And the money's just a gesture really, to cover costs. What you did for us can never be repaid.'

The sailors hadn't even signed the note, or left a forwarding address. Aunty screwed it up. You could see how offended she was that they'd gone off like that. She even screwed up the money and went to chuck it in the bin.

But Uncle wouldn't let her. 'That's life,' he said. 'They'll have meant no harm. They just weren't thinking. Besides, when could we afford to throw good money away?'

He flattened out the money and stuck it in one of the cups for when they needed a bit of spare cash. Aunty put them on the top shelf of the kitchen cabinet, where she kept things she never used. In the days and weeks that followed, she never talked about the sailors again or the strange way they'd come bursting into their lives. You'd have thought she had forgotten them, and Uncle had as well.

But Mad Dog thought about them all the time, and wondered who they were.

Part II
Devil's Bridge

7

The Aged Relative

Some people burned bright, it seemed, then simply disappeared. They came into your life and then went again, and there was nothing you could do but stand by and watch. Mad Dog's parents, for example, and now the sailors.

Ever afterwards, there was something about those sailors that wouldn't let Mad Dog go. He mightn't know their names or anything else about them, but they'd come bursting into his life bringing stories of other places far away – of other worlds, and other ways of looking at the world. And even years after they'd gone, Mad Dog dreamt about their wide horizons and journeys without ending, and imagined himself a sailor just like them, travelling across seas that might be cruel but could never subdue him, meeting mermaids, discovering lost continents, chasing dolphins and cruising across silver seas. The rest of his life was dominated by mundane things like school and lessons and routine. But at least, as he grew up, he had other things to dream about.

He was growing bigger all the time, and so was Elvis, who'd turned into a tough but friendly little lad, coming home from playing with his friends with scraped knees and glorious tales of fights. Mad Dog was proud of him. Aunty wasn't so impressed, but he reckoned he could see his brother's Trojan blood coming out in him. Nothing more was said about adoption, not since the day they'd sworn on the Bible, but neither was there any mention of leaving the Gap.

No. 3 was their home, and Aunty and Uncle were their parents in all but name. The past was set aside as if it had never been. The *ffon* languished in the wardrobe, its secret message forgotten. Mad Dog was embarrassed about those old days when he'd talked to his walking cane as if it was a person. Only five-year-olds did things like that. And besides, he didn't need secrets to feel like a person who mattered. He didn't even need parents. Life was fine the way it was.

And it remained fine too, until one February morning, the beginning of half-term week, when Mad Dog came downstairs to find Aunty on the phone and everything about to change. In total ignorance of what was happening, he went out to play on the barge den, only to come back later and find Aunty and her sisters huddled in the kitchen. Their heads were knit together and their voices were raised as one in indignation – which meant there could be only one person they were talking about.

The Aged Relative.

Mad Dog didn't know exactly who the Aged Relative was, and he didn't care if he never found out. He'd only spoken to her once, and that had been enough, picking up the phone when no one was about, only for a cold voice to bark at him, 'I don't want *you*. God, what's wrong with the world? Why are children allowed to answer phones? I want to talk to your aunt.'

Sometimes Aunty or one of her sisters would visit the Aged Relative, going with long faces and coming back with even longer ones. At times like Christmas there'd be discussions about having her to stay but, despite their best-laid plans, she'd either refuse to come or pull out at the last minute. Now some sort of crisis seemed to be taking place, because Luke's mum was saying, 'It's always the same,' and Hippie's mum was saying, 'When *we* need help, she's never there for *us*,' and Rhys's mum was telling Aunty, wagging her finger as she did so, 'You leave well alone. If she's got into a mess, it'll be of her own making. However much you do for her, it'll never be enough. But she tries it on with you because she thinks you're a soft touch.'

Unfortunately for Mad Dog, the advice wasn't taken. Aunty flared up at the suggestion that she was a soft touch and said that her sisters weren't being fair, either to her or the Aged Relative who – just this once – appeared to have a genuine grievance. Her sisters snorted and said, 'Since when?'

Aunty didn't answer, but when Uncle came in for lunch, he found her packing the car. 'Where are you going?' he asked, and didn't look very pleased about it when Aunty told him.

'You can't take children to a place like that,' he said.

'What else am I to do?' said Aunty. 'Are you going to take time off work and look after them? I don't think so. And my beloved sisters certainly aren't going to.'

She was in a foul mood, and it didn't get any better when they'd set off. All the way through Aberystwyth she banged the steering wheel and cursed as if no one else had a right on the road. Usually she was such a careful driver, but today she kept beeping her horn and changing lanes without indicating.

They left the town behind and started down the coast road. The sun was shining and Mad Dog's hopes began to rise. Perhaps the Aged Relative would turn out to live in a bungalow by the sea with a beach nearby where he and Elvis could go and play, which meant that, however horrible she was, they could always get out of her way.

A few miles down the road, however, Aunty took a sharp turn inland, leaving the sea behind and heading up into the hills. The road she'd chosen went up and down like a fairground switchback and Mad Dog started feeling carsick. He tried to focus his eyes on the way ahead, but dizzying glimpses of sheer drops and the valley floor beneath him didn't help.

'How much further?' he kept on asking.

'Not far now,' Aunty would reply.

It felt far to Mad Dog – especially after Aunty took a wrong turning and had to retrace their journey for several miles. Finally, however, the car plunged down into woodland, and the outskirts of a village came into view. They passed an empty railway station with a sign announcing that it was closed until Easter; a general store; a campsite set in a sunless wood; a tourist shop that had been boarded up; a series of old bridges, each built over the other and set back amongst woodland; and a tumbling waterfall that appeared to be the village's main tourist attraction but couldn't be got down to without going through a turnstile and paying money.

The waterfall was at the lowest part of the village, set next to a rather grand-looking hotel. Once past it, the car crawled its way up a series of hairpin bends until Aunty pulled sharply left on to a gravel drive. Here a grey stone house loomed into view, its paintwork peeling, its gate hanging off its hinges, weeds growing up its path.

'Well, here we are,' Aunty said with a sigh.

She switched off the engine and got straight out of the car as if afraid of changing her mind if she hesitated. Mad Dog got out too, and immediately the sound of running water rushed to greet him from a cliff that stood behind the house. Everything was cast in its shadow. The house. The garden. Even the sign by the hanging gate.

THE DEVIL'S BRIDGE B & B it said, and, hand-written underneath it, in capital letters, underlined heavily, were the words:

<u>NO VACANCIES</u>

8

The Man with Red Tattoos

It didn't take a man with red tattoos all over his chest to convince Mad Dog that the Devil's Bridge B & B was not a place where he wanted to spend his half-term holiday. But the man didn't help. Before they'd even got up the path, he'd materialised in the porch as if by magic and stood, hands on hips, shirt open, silver charms around his neck, glaring down at them, his hair as red as danger, his eyes as black as wrinkled prunes.

It was as if they'd no right to be there. Aunty waved for him to come and help them with the luggage, but he took no notice and they had to manage on their own.

'We have a room booked,' Aunty said when she reached the porch.

The man refused to get out of her way. She stood right in front of him, but he wouldn't budge. 'You must have got that wrong,' he said. 'We've been closed since before Christmas.' He pointed down to the NO VACANCIES sign as if to say *can't you read?*

'But I booked a room only a couple of hours ago,' Aunty insisted. 'And the person I spoke to didn't say anything about being closed.'

She pushed the man aside and entered the B & B, dragging Mad Dog and Elvis behind her. Mad Dog never forgot the smell of boiled cabbage as he passed the man. The hall in which he found himself was dark, with yellowing wallpaper. He shivered, wishing that Aunty had booked them into the hotel down the road. He couldn't understand what they were doing here in this horrid B & B, and, for the first time in ages, he thought about his *ffon* and wished he had it with him to keep him safe.

By now Aunty had located the reception 'desk' – a small square hatch in the wall that looked as if it hadn't been opened for years. Positioning herself in front of it, she pressed a bell that set off a piercing scream all over the house. With a sigh of annoyance, the tattooed man disappeared through a door behind them, then reappeared behind the hatch.

'Look, you're not down in the register,' he said, opening out a dusty-looking ledger with nothing written in it.

'I don't care what I may or may not be down in,' Aunty said. 'If you don't take me to my room, I'll call the Manager.'

'I *am* the Manager,' the man said.

Aunty looked him up and down. 'Oh yes?' she said. 'Then show me to my room or else I'll call the owner instead.'

It was obvious she wasn't going to back down. The Manager stared at her with all the friendliness of a cornered dog. He pushed the book at her and she signed her name, then he led them upstairs to a sunless room which was cold even by February's standards, and dominated by the sound of running water.

At first Mad Dog thought there must be a leak somewhere, but then he realised that the sound came from the rock face immediately outside their window. He turned towards Aunty, who was busy examining cobwebs that hung in strings across the ceiling and dots of black mould on the wallpaper.

'You can't seriously expect us to stay in here?' she said.

'This is the only room that isn't closed for redecoration,' the Manager said, and turned and left them to it.

Mad Dog wished that he could leave as well. He wished that Aunty would tell the Manager where to stick his room. But all she did was take a few quick photos on her mobile phone – although what for Mad Dog couldn't imagine – then start the process of making things more comfortable.

First she found an electric fire and switched it on, then she went down to the reception area and came back with hot-water bottles to air the beds, dusters, spray-can polish and even a vacuum cleaner. Then she got stuck in.

Mad Dog couldn't understand why she was bothering. None of it made sense. Even he – with his limited knowledge of the world – understood that if you booked into a B & B you weren't meant to do your own cleaning. But Aunty did it all, and afterwards she dug a kettle out of the back of the wardrobe and brewed them all a cup of tea.

Mad Dog didn't like tea, but given how cold he was he drank it anyway. The three of them sat facing each other on the edges of their beds. Their coats hung on the back of the door. Their shoes lined up along the wall. Their clothes were unpacked into the wardrobe, and the room still mightn't look remotely homely but Aunty had done her best.

'So, when are we going to see the Aged Relative?'

Mad Dog said.

Aunty shrugged. 'When I'm ready,' she said – whatever that meant.

'And when will that be?' Mad Dog said.

This time Aunty didn't even answer. Other things plainly were on her mind. After they'd finished their tea, she led them off on a tour round the rest of the house, opening doors and looking round them, poking into corners, tutting over what she found, taking more photographs and writing things down in a little notebook that she kept digging out of her handbag.

Mad Dog was worried about the Manager catching them out, but Aunty said she couldn't care less. When they'd finished with the bedrooms – which might be closed for redecoration, but there was precious little to be seen of it – she took them downstairs to see the dining room.

This turned out to be a grubby pink-and-blue box of a room with chairs on tables, which looked as if it hadn't been used for years. Aunty poked her way round it, looking in drawers and counting plates and silver cutlery, then led them through the kitchen, where she did the same.

Finally they even found their way into the office, which lay behind the reception hatch. Mad Dog expected the Manager to come leaping out and chase them away, but he wasn't anywhere to be seen. Having failed to keep them out, it seemed, he'd simply given up.

It was only on their way back to their room that they came across him. Aunty heard a piano being played somewhere and insisted on going to investigate. And there, in a dusty old conservatory at the back of the house, amid stacked-up chairs and trestle tables, an empty counter with a tea urn, and an old box-freezer for Lyons Maid ice cream, they found the Manager playing tunes from a stack of yellowing sheet music held together with Sellotape.

'Some Enchanted Evening' he played, smiling to himself as if at some private joke, singing along as if he didn't know that anyone was watching.

Mad Dog shivered. He really didn't like this Manager. There was something about him that went deeper than mere grumpiness. Something he couldn't put his finger on but, if he'd been Aunty, he'd have turned tail and gone.

Aunty, however, had no intention of going anywhere. 'I'm hungry,' she announced. 'We all are. We've been looking for you everywhere. Could you find us something to eat?'

The Manager closed the piano. When he turned his face towards them, the smile had gone, replaced by an expression of perfect blankness. He said that the Devil's Bridge B & B didn't 'do' food any more and the dining room was closed until further notice.

But Aunty wouldn't have it. Mad Dog had never seen her so determined. She was a pretty strong-minded woman normally but, ever since coming here to Devil's Bridge, her strong-mindedness had moved into a whole new league.

Now she said she wanted food, and had no doubt that, if he applied himself, the Manager could 'do something about it'. The Manager didn't like it, but Aunty wouldn't back down and, in the end – with her threatening to take over his kitchen – he agreed to 'rustle something up'.

When their meal arrived, however, Mad Dog rather wished the Manager hadn't bothered. He forced down tinned tomato soup heated to lukewarm, boiled haddock that was cold in the middle, sliced white bread, a mound of soggy cabbage, and mashed bananas served with lumpy custard and tinned cream.

It wasn't the worst meal Mad Dog had ever eaten – that honour went to Hippie's mum with her lentils and mung beans – but it wasn't far off. All the way through it, Mad Dog poked his food around his plate and waited for Aunty to complain. But she didn't say a word and he wondered what was wrong with her.

Back in their room afterwards, Aunty brushed her teeth as if trying to get rid of the taste of fish, washed her face, combed her hair and even applied a little make-up. Then she made Mad Dog and Elvis change into clean clothes, including their best shoes.

'What's going on?' Mad Dog said.

'It's time to meet the Aged Relative,' Aunty said.

The Aged Relative! *At last!* Wondering what they were in for, Mad Dog followed Aunty downstairs again. Here she rang the terrible bell at the reception hatch. She didn't take her finger off until a plainly rattled Manager appeared, dressed in pyjamas as if he'd already retired for the night. As it wasn't even eight o'clock, Aunty looked surprised. Her voice laced with sarcasm, she announced that she was sorry to disturb him but needed to speak to the owner.

The Manager looked as if he'd had enough. 'I'm the owner,' he said.

'No, you said you were the Manager,' Aunty said.

'You heard wrong. I said I was the owner,' the Manager said.

Aunty smiled. Mad Dog didn't like her smile, and he'd have liked it even less if he'd been in the Manager's shoes.

'Oh, I heard wrong, did I?' she said. 'You're the owner, are you? Well, I think not. I'd know her if I saw her, as I'm sure you will agree. After all, I ought to know my own *mother*, don't you think?'

9

Up and Running

If there'd been a competition for who was more astounded, the winner would have been hard to pick. The Manager's mouth fell open with obvious surprise, while Mad Dog's mind raced through a thousand questions, all to do with how Aunty could have a mother without him realising it – especially one as sour and unfriendly as the Aged Relative.

'I'm sorry, but could you repeat that?' he heard the Manager say somewhere in what felt like the distance.

'If you don't mind, I'd like to see my mother,' Aunty said.

The Manager got it remarkably quickly. Mad Dog was still struggling to put the whole thing together, as if it were a sum whose parts he stood a chance of understanding. Owner of hotel plus Aged Relative equals what – Aunty's mother? Surely not!

But throwing Aunty a glance that acknowledged the extent to which he'd underestimated her, the Manager said, 'I see. Well, if you'd explained when you arrived, I'd have understood. But I do now, and I'll take you to her. She'll be pleased to see you, I'm sure. Come this way.'

In an exhibition of control that was impressive to observe, he led them back upstairs, then upstairs again to a long attic landing with doors off it. Here they passed through a fire door and came to what had to be the remotest room in the house. The Manager rapped on the door.

'What do you want?' a thin voice barked from inside the room.

The Manager didn't answer, just turned the handle and stepped aside, an expression on his face that could have crushed cars. The door swung open and Aunty walked in, followed by Elvis and then by Mad Dog – only to find themselves confronted by an enormous four-poster bed.

The three of them stood before it, looking up. At first Mad Dog didn't realise what it was, only that some sort of massive frame with curtains pulled round it filled the room and blocked his going any further. Only when he caught a glimpse of pillows behind the curtains did it occur to him that it might be a bed. And then he couldn't imagine how anybody could get in or out of it, not without a ladder.

'Mother, it's me,' Aunty called. 'You must be up there somewhere. Show yourself.'

Something rustled behind the curtains, then a great grey dog stuck out a face that was dappled with pale red spots as if it was getting over chicken pox. Acting the role of guardian of the bed, it issued a low, throaty growl which brought another dog to join it and then a third.

Mad Dog took a step back, getting behind Aunty and wishing yet again that he'd got his *ffon* with him. Elvis stepped back too, but Aunty stood her ground.

'Mother,' she said. 'This is ridiculous. I know you're up there.'

Something moved behind the dogs – a shifting of curtains that allowed a tiny face to peer down. 'What do you want?' said a sour, unfriendly voice that Mad

Dog recalled immediately from that time on the phone.

'I don't want anything,' said Aunty. 'I'm here because you asked for me. Remember?'

The Aged Relative's face screwed up into a tight red ball and her eyes blinked quickly as if she was flustered.

'I don't know what you're talking about,' she said. 'Of course I didn't ask for you. Why would I do that? Don't be ridiculous.'

She tried to hide herself behind the curtains, but Aunty wouldn't let her, pulling them back to reveal an old woman with dyed beige hair, skin as grey as if it never saw the light of day and a grubby-looking nightdress that looked as if it hadn't been changed for weeks. The only thing about the Aged Relative that wasn't shabby was a handful of gold rings studded with enormous stones that looked like diamonds, emeralds and rubies.

Mad Dog stared at them. He'd never seen such big jewels in his life. Everything else about the Aged Relative was colourless, but her rings shone like fire.

The Aged Relative saw where Mad Dog was looking and thrust her hands under the covers. 'What's *he* doing here?' she snapped. 'And the other one. I won't have children in my B & B. You know that. Pets, yes, but children, no. It's all there in the brochure.'

'What brochure?' Aunty said. She pushed the dogs away and hauled herself on to the bed to confront her mother face to face. 'In fact, what B & B? There isn't one that I've yet seen. Just some empty ruin of a house. And on that subject ...'

Before she could say any more, the Manager entered the room.

'Is there anything I can get you?' he said, putting on a show of concern that had been completely lacking in anything he'd done so far.

If the Aged Relative had been a princess, and he her humble servant, he couldn't have treated her better. He cleared away a stack of plates and ordered the dogs to get off the bed. They obeyed him immediately, slinking out of the room after glaring resentfully at Aunty, Mad Dog and Elvis.

Mad Dog expected the Manager to follow them, but he remained fussing around, and it was only when Aunty said, 'Do you mind? I'm trying to have a private talk with my mother,' that he finally went.

'And don't come back,' Aunty said, slamming the door behind him.

'You shouldn't have done that,' the Aged Relative said.

'And how exactly should I treat a man who's taking advantage of my mother?' Aunty said.

The Aged Relative blinked again as if she was even more flustered than before. 'You don't understand – *walls have ears*,' she whispered.

Aunty laughed at that. You could see how much the Manager had got under her skin. 'Good!' she said. 'Then they can hear what I have to say, which is that you bought this B & B against all our advice, which means it's yours and no one else's and you should take responsibility for it, not lie around in bed watching telly all the time, or whatever it is you do. I know you, Mother. I know what you're like. When was the last time you went downstairs? The last time you checked the register? The last time you went into the kitchen, or ordered food for your guests, or even had any guests? When was the last time you paid your bills? Do you know what's going on in your own house? You don't have a clue, do you?'

Aunty pulled out her notepad and started reading. But, like a child being scolded, the Aged Relative put her hands over her ears. Then Aunty dug out her phone to show her some of the pictures she'd taken. But the Aged Relative picked up the remote control and turned on the telly that sat at the end of her bed.

'It's my favourite programme,' she said, 'I've been waiting for it all day.'

Aunty turned bright red. 'If you don't listen to me,' she said, 'I'll leave right now and not come back. I'm not just saying this – I mean it. If I count for less than the telly, I'll take Ryan and Eric – who've got better things to do, believe me, than hang around here – and leave. And then whatever was so important that you phoned in tears, pleading for me to come, will never get dealt with. Not by me, *so help me God*.'

The two women glared at each other, mother and daughter, so different and yet, in some respects, so uncannily alike. For a moment neither moved – then the Aged Relative switched the telly up louder.

'I've always been scared of you,' she said petulantly. 'You're such a bully. You always have been ever since you were a little girl.'

Aunty sighed, her exasperation complete. 'Well, you would know,' she said. 'When it comes to bullying, you wear the crown.'

And that was it. The end of their audience with the Aged Relative. They left the room. On the way out,

Aunty tossed the notepad up on to the bed – not, she said, because she expected her mother to ever bother reading it, but because she, Aunty, wanted to know in the long years to come that she'd tried her best.

Back in their room, they packed to leave. Aunty's expression was one of relief. 'I should feel sorry for her,' she said, 'but she's got what she's been asking for. She's a lazy, selfish woman who's always expected other people to do her dirty work for her. And now she's had her come-uppance. That so-called "manager" of hers might be running around her when there's someone to witness him in action, but he's also bleeding her dry – and she's got no one to blame for it but herself. We told her, all of us, that buying a B & B was a crazy idea. But would she listen? Would she hell!'

Once they were packed, they made their way downstairs. It was ten thirty at night, time for climbing into bed and going to sleep, but none of them wanted to stay. Aunty packed the car. They all piled into it and were just about to drive off when the porch door banged open, and the Aged Relative appeared, swaying as if the effort of standing on her own legs was proving a bit much.

'You can't go!' she wailed. 'I'm not a well person! It's my dicky heart. I need help! Surely you can see that. I need you. I'm frightened. Don't leave me! *Not with him!*'

Aunty stayed. It was the *not with him* that was the clincher. How could she leave after a plea like that? The three of them unpacked again, and spent the night in beds that sank in the middle and felt damp even after airing with hot water-bottles. Mad Dog felt like a prisoner who'd tried to make a run for it but failed. The prisoner of the Aged Relative – and you could see her crowing as if she thought she'd got power over them all.

But the real power, it was quite obvious to Mad Dog, belonged to the Manager. For the rest of the week Aunty attempted to get him working but he refused to do a thing. She issued him with lists of jobs but he kept on disappearing, leaving her to do everything. And every time she complained, the Aged Relative stuck up for him.

Mad Dog didn't get it. Neither did Aunty. If the Aged Relative was as frightened of the Manager as she appeared to be, then why wasn't she seizing the opportunity of having someone else around to tackle him? It just didn't make sense.

In the meantime, however, there were gutters to clear, windows to wash, food to be bought in, accounts to be examined and a house to be cleaned that looked as if it hadn't been touched in years. Aunty tried getting the Aged Relative to help, but she was as good at getting out of it as the Manager, always using her weak legs and 'dicky heart' as her excuse.

By the end of the week, Aunty was exhausted. So was Mad Dog, who'd done his best to help, but had had enough. They all had. On their last night, over dinner in the dining room, Aunty tried one last time to persuade the Aged Relative not only to get rid of the Manager but the house as well, and move into a little flat which would be easier to look after.

But the Aged Relative wouldn't hear of it. 'If you and your sisters looked after me properly,' she said, fixing Aunty with a sour eye, 'everything would be all right. Then there'd be no manager and I could do this on my own. This is all your fault. You should be running this place between you, not leaving me to my own devices. I'm your mother and you owe me.'

Aunty turned pale at that. 'Owe you for what, Mother?' she said in a still, small voice.

For a moment, you could have cut the atmosphere with a knife. Then the Manager's dogs came bounding in and stood around the table looking just about as threatening as a cohort of Republican Guards. Aunty shouted at them to go away, but they refused to budge and wouldn't even move for the Aged Relative.

'Honestly, Mother, can't you even control your own dogs?' Aunty said.

'They're not mine. They're *his*,' the Aged Relative said.

Aunty sighed. That man again. 'Of all the people you could have chosen to work for you, why did you have to pick him?' she said.

'I didn't pick him. He just turned up. In fact, you could say *he* picked *me*,' the Aged Relative said.

'Yes, but you must have some idea of who he is, where he comes from, where he's worked before?' Aunty said. 'He must have references. You must know something.'

'I don't know anything,' the Aged Relative said. 'Except that now you're walking out on me, I'll need him all the more.'

10

The Manager's Ball

This time, when the bags were packed, Mad Dog knew Aunty wouldn't change her mind. Sure enough, she went to bed, saying she couldn't wait for the morning when they'd be off, and slept like a baby.

Mad Dog wished that he could sleep too, but tossed and turned, unable to get comfortable. He longed for morning and wished they could have left already. Even after cleaning up the house, he didn't like it. It was bad enough by day, but in the dark the sound of running water outside seemed to be magnified and the walls and floorboards seemed to creak as if people were sneaking about.

Every night Mad Dog reckoned he could hear muffled sounds, as if people were whispering outside his door, but tonight it was worse than ever. He told himself that all houses made noises in the darkness, including No. 3, but tonight he was sure he could hear doors opening and closing, and the swish of dresses going down the corridor, and even snatches of music.

In the end, determined to find out what was going on, Mad Dog went to investigate. Creeping along the landing, he was convinced that, at worst, he'd find a radio left on somewhere, or the Manager watching a bit of late-night telly. At the top of the stairs, he looked down into the darkness. There was not a soul about, but the sound of music rose up to greet him, followed by a murmur of voices. It didn't sound like the telly, but it *did* sound like a party. Not an imaginary one, either. A real party.

Mad Dog tiptoed downstairs, his curiosity aroused. Down in the hall, it seemed to him that the sound was coming from the conservatory. He slipped outside, sneaked round the back of the house and, sure enough, there beyond the kitchen, he found the conservatory windows ablaze with light.

That was the moment when Mad Dog should have gone back for Aunty. Instead, however, under cover of darkness, he crept up to the windows to see what was going on. Last time he'd seen inside the conservatory there'd been chairs and tables stacked everywhere. But now someone had cleared them away, brushed down all the cobwebs and placed tall black candles on all the window sills.

Not only that, but they'd invited in an array of glittering guests.

The conservatory was full of them. Mad Dog stood in the darkness, watching them dancing past the windows in black frocks and white ties, black coats, white silk scarves, black plumes, white diamonds, black jet earrings, sequinned masks and feathered fans. Every man was a peacock, every woman a dancing queen.

Mad Dog couldn't believe what he was seeing. A ball was taking place in the Aged Relative's conservatory, and she didn't know a thing about it. The windows were open and Mad Dog felt its heat. The conservatory felt like an oven, but the only person who seemed unaffected by it was the Manager, seated at the piano, driving the dancers with his playing.

When Mad Dog saw him, it took all his courage not to turn and flee. In the candlelight the Manager's hair blazed like fire, and his hands on the piano moved up and down so fast that they almost looked like smoke. The guests whirled past as if he held them in his thrall, and even Mad Dog found himself wanting to join in.

Against his will, his toes tapped, his head bobbed and the rhythm of the music soaked into him. The music was so powerful that he nearly found himself throwing caution to the winds and leaping in through the window. It beat that hard and it really swung.

But then, as the dancers whirled around the room, masks started slipping and faces started showing through – pinched, taut faces, their expressions filled with what almost looked like panic. It was as if they were prisoners behind their masks. As if they were caught up in something that they couldn't stop.

For it wasn't just the music that drove them on. There were other faces on that dance floor – grey, grim faces behind their masks that looked more like guards than party-goers. In fact more like dogs than human dancers – *more like the dogs who guarded the Aged Relative's bed!*

Mad Dog cried out. Immediately everybody turned towards the window, including the Manager, who stopped playing. Everybody saw Mad Dog there and, for a moment, he expected the Manager to set his dogs on him.

But then the Manager laughed, as if his presence out there in the darkness was a joke. He turned away and started playing again. And again the beat was irresistible and again the dancers started whirling round.

Mad Dog felt as if the Manager was saying, '*Look at me. Look what I can do. I'm in charge. These people are mine.*' The last he saw of them, they were whirling faster than before, sweat pouring off them. By this time the Manager was sweating too, his shirt slashed open to the waist, revealing yet more red tattoos running up and down his body like a road map drawn in blood, and the chain around his throat packed with silver charms.

Mad Dog shivered at the sight of that chain, but didn't know why. He turned and fled, racing back round the house as if trying to escape some weird dance of death. In through the front door he ran, tearing across the reception area and back upstairs, taking endless wrong turnings in his panic but eventually making it back to his bedroom, where he shook Aunty awake.

'We've got to leave! We've got to go! It's the Manager! We've got to get out of here *right now!*'

Aunty wouldn't go, of course. She was made of sterner stuff than that. Instead she went downstairs to see what was going on. By the time she reached the conservatory, however, the dance was over and the room stood empty. She walked around it, examining everything for evidence of mischief, but the heat had died down and even the black candles had disappeared.

Mad Dog didn't tell her about the dogs in coats and party frocks, reckoning she'd never believe him. But he did tell her about the other guests, and the Manager's part in it all, and she did find a bit of hot wax on a window sill and a few empty bottles shut under the piano lid.

'Well, I'd say it looks like somebody's been celebrating

our departure,' she said. 'Though a bit too early, if you ask me. And it doesn't take much to guess who.'

Next morning, after making a showy farewell to the Aged Relative and driving off noisily with a car full of children and luggage, Aunty parked down the road and sneaked back. She told Mad Dog and Elvis to stay where they were and not follow her. But, after waiting a couple of minutes, they were too curious to do anything else.

By the time they arrived at the hotel, Aunty had already come across the Manager – whose sudden emergence after a week of lying low was, she put to him, no coincidence – and had him in a corner like a rat in a shed. Mad Dog feared for her, wondering if she had any idea what she was dealing with.

'Don't think I'm ignorant of what's been going on,' she said. 'And I'm not just talking about parties. I'm talking about the way you've got my mother under your thumb. Well, I want you out, and I want it now – you and your dogs with you. In fact, I'm not going anywhere until I've seen the last of you. And don't think you're going to appeal to my mother over my head because – contrary to what she may have told you – *she wants you out as well!*'

Aunty meant it about not going anywhere. She'd have stayed there for the next hundred years if she'd had to. Mad Dog waited for the Manager to call down bolts of lightning upon Aunty's head, but instead he slunk off to his quarters as if he was defeated.

It didn't take him long to pack – but then he didn't have much to take with him. Mad Dog watched him reappear, his dogs at his heel, an old coat thrown on and buttoned up to his throat. The Manager was licked, and he knew it. Mad Dog marvelled that he'd ever been frightened of this manky creature with his flashy charm necklace, and horrible tattoos.

But even so, as the Manager walked out, Mad Dog still found himself shivering as if the shadow of another world had briefly touched his own. And Elvis shivered as if he felt it too, and clung to Mad Dog's side. And even Aunty shivered as the Manager passed her by.

Then he was gone, heading down the drive without a word to any of them, taking his dogs with him. At the road he turned back to give them a final dagger's glance. Then he disappeared, and a burst of song could be heard upstairs in the house. It was as if even the Aged Relative recognised that something bad had passed out of their lives.

11

A Poisoned Chalice

Within the week, the Aged Relative was dead. Mad Dog scarcely had time to savour being home again when he returned from school one afternoon to find Aunty on the phone making funeral arrangements. Her face was as white as a sheet and her voice sounded strange and tight. The Aged Relative had been found dead by the woman from the post office out walking her dog. It had been a cold, crisp morning and the Aged Relative had been covered in frost as if she'd been out there all night, sitting on a bench in her garden, the property pages of the local newspaper spread out around her, several flats and bungalows circled in green ink.

'I never believed her,' Aunty said. 'But she *did* have a dicky heart after all. And I was there. I saw what she was like, and I thought she hammed it up for sympathy. I feel so ashamed.'

The funeral service was held in the church at Parson's Bridge, which was up the valley from the Aged Relative's now defunct B & B. The sisters all attended, dressed in deepest black and wearing expressions to match. Afterwards a lunch of drinks and snacks was served in the dining room, and everybody looked at everybody else, all secretly wondering the same thing – how the Aged Relative had decided to dispose of her estate.

They didn't have to wait long to find out. After

lunch, the Aged Relative's solicitor appeared, and read out her Last Will and Testament. All the children were sent out to play, but none of them went far, hanging round the garden as if they knew that something special was happening indoors.

The general feeling seemed to be that the Aged Relative was a secret millionairess. Luke said his mum reckoned she had Rolls-Royce cars stashed away, and properties in the south of France. Mad Dog told them all about the Aged Relative's jewelled rings. Hippie said that if his mum inherited any money she was going to spend it setting up a Buddhist retreat. The only one who sounded a note of caution was Rhys, whose mum was certain that the Aged Relative would leave her secret millions to the local donkey sanctuary to spite them all.

She wasn't far wrong either, at least about the spiting bit. The sisters came out arguing, cut off without a penny – all except for Aunty, who had inherited the lot.

The Aged Relative had done it on purpose, of course. Her Will was meant to set them at each other's throats – and it had worked perfectly. The arguments rolled on for days, on the phone and in each other's kitchens, the general feeling being that Aunty had slyly weaseled her way into everybody else's inheritance.

Along the Gap, the atmosphere was electric. Aunty, angry and hurt, announced that the Aged Relative's money was tainted and she wouldn't take a penny of it. In fact, she'd share it round and leave herself out. But her sisters wouldn't have it. The Aged Relative had referred to them in her Will as a 'worthless bunch' and they were mortally offended.

So Aunty was in the money, and there was nothing she could do about it. She owned a house. She had, if not a Rolls-Royce, at least a beaten up old Range Rover. She had money in the bank. She even had the gold rings – which, though not as valuable as they looked, were still worth what Uncle called 'a bob or two'.

Uncle said that an injection of cash never went amiss and that Aunty should cheer up and make the most of it. But Aunty couldn't see it that way. He said that this bequest was her chance to make something of herself.

'It isn't a bequest,' Aunty said. 'It's a *poisoned chalice.*'

They were up at Devil's Bridge at the time, taking a long hard look at the Aged Relative's house and deciding what to do with it. Aunty wanted to get rid of it, and as quickly as possible, and Mad Dog agreed with her, but Uncle saw things differently.

'It's not just a house, it's an investment,' he said. 'It might look gloomy now, but if we did it up we could put it on the market and make a whacking profit. It wouldn't take much. Just a few repairs and a lick of paint.'

Aunty was persuaded – but lived to wonder what she'd done. Once the repairs had got under way, walls were found in need of shoring up. Broken wiring had to be ripped out. Plaster crumbled at a touch. Pipes leaked and had to be replaced. Floorboards were found to be rotting and roof joists sagged, costing a small fortune to repair.

In the end, the 'few repairs' took more than a year to do and involved architects, builders and a structural engineer. Once started, it seemed, there could be no going back. The sisters called the project Aunty's 'folly' but Uncle continued to insist that it was an investment.

He was right too, because once the house was in a good enough state to put on the market, it sold with extraordinary ease. No sooner had the estate agent's photographs gone into the newspapers, than people started phoning up. And, no sooner had the first of them been to see it, driving all the way from London, than Aunty found herself with an offer that she couldn't refuse.

Everyone was astonished, including Aunty's sisters, who said that they were pleased for her – but didn't look it. A firm of flashy architects turned up at the London people's request to work out how to turn the house into a luxury hotel, complete with hot tubs and a swimming pool. A completion date was agreed for contracts to be signed and Aunty got on with a string of last-minute jobs that she'd promised to do before handing over.

It was around this time that Mad Dog started noticing a change in Aunty. Once, when they'd been working on the house, she'd insisted on only having bare essentials around them. But now it seemed that half their clothes had worked their way up there, not to say anything of half their books, CDs, toys, cooking pots, a portable TV and even a couple of family photographs that appeared one day, hanging on the wall to make the place look 'homelier'.

Why they'd want a house that they were selling anyway to feel homelier, Mad Dog couldn't imagine. But, by the time a sofa had worked its way up there too, along with a couple of armchairs and even some spare curtains, Mad Dog was beginning to feel alarm bells ringing.

Another change he noticed was in Aunty's attitude towards her neighbours. In the early days, she hadn't been interested in making friends, but now she was even trying to make them for him too. The girl who lived down at the post office was his age apparently and seemed 'very nice', and so did the boy in the stone house next to the railway station, and another boy whose parents owned a holiday cottage next to the big hotel.

'We should invite them round,' said Aunty. 'Get to know them. What do you think?'

Mad Dog said he didn't want to get to know new people, especially in a place they'd sold and weren't ever to see again. Aunty said she understood, but that didn't stop her making friends of her own. She even invited all these new friends to the party she'd decided to throw the day before signing over the house.

Mad Dog worried about this party. Something about it set alarm bells ringing too. The whole village was invited and so was everybody back in the Gap. Aunty worked her fingers to the bone, anxious to show the world what she'd achieved. The night before the party, she was up until the early hours preparing food.

By the time the first guests were arriving next day, everything was in a state of perfect readiness, right down to the last leaf chased off the lawn. Aunty looked happy and relaxed, waiting for her sisters to come and see that what she'd achieved wasn't a folly after all.

But they never came. First one and then another phoned with apologies, saying they couldn't make it. Aunty took it personally, of course, but Uncle said he wasn't surprised. All year long they'd refused to come up and see what she'd done.

'It's their loss,' he said. 'Don't get upset. The rest of us are going to have a great party without them. And you're going to have a great party too. You deserve it. You mustn't let your sisters spoil your day.'

True to his word, the party was a huge success. All the new friends from the village arrived in force, along with most of Uncle's side of the family and a couple of wild-card Williamses who'd only come, Aunty reckoned, to report back to the sisters. The London people turned up too, having been invited to meet their new neighbours, and Aunty was in her element, serving mountains of food and making it all look effortless.

When the supper had been cleared away, a band set up and everybody danced. The London people declared themselves delighted with the village into which they were buying. At the end of the evening they even made a speech about it, flushed and excited, talking about feeling part of the community already. Then the post office lady's husband – who was a local councillor – made a speech in which he said that community life came with responsibilities and he hoped the London people would feel free to muck in with the rest of them.

Then it was Aunty's turn for a speech. Worn out with hard work by this time, and flushed with just a little bit too much white wine, she got to her feet.

'Thank you all for coming,' she said, looking round at them all. 'It's been a great night and a great end to a strange and unexpected period of my life. I scarcely can believe how much things have changed since Mother died. How much this house has changed as well. It's been hard work all the way, but worth it.

'What I'm showing off tonight bears no resemblance to what I started out with. And how I feel about it bears no resemblance either. At the time, the words I used for my bequest were *poisoned chalice*. I wished I'd never seen this house. And yet now I'm proud of it.

'You builders have done a great job, and you architects, electricians, plumbers and engineers too. And you, our friends here in the village, have done a great job too, giving us support which has been much needed. So thank you, all of you. But don't think you've seen the last of us – *because you haven't*.'

Aunty swayed on her feet. Everybody was staring at her. They plainly didn't have a clue what was coming next. Not even Uncle knew. But Mad Dog did. Suddenly he knew what all those warning bells had been about!

'Tonight,' Aunty carried on, beaming round at all of them, 'tonight, for the first time, I can see something I should have realised long ago. This thing that I've inherited here – it isn't just a house. It's a place as well, and it's the people in it. Over the past few months, you've all become a part of me. Once I never would have thought it, but now this house feels like home. And that's why I've decided *not to sell after all*.'

You could have heard a pin drop. Mad Dog looked round the room. Everybody was staring at Aunty, including the London people whose smiles were frozen on their faces. But Aunty only had eyes for Uncle, whose whole face had formed itself into a silent, *Whaaat …?*

'What I mean,' Aunty said, looking at him directly as if no one else mattered, 'is that I simply can't go through with it. And I don't see why I should. What have I got waiting for me down in the Gap? My sisters don't want me, so why am I selling up? It makes no sense. I mean, if someone else can turn our beautifully restored property into a money-spinning country-house hotel, then why not have a go ourselves? You know – test the water and see how we get on. We mightn't be able to afford hot tubs and a swimming pool and things like that. But I could run the kitchen, and you could run the bar and we've just about got enough money to take on a couple of staff. We could make a go of it. I'm sure we could. I know we've never done anything like this before, but we've just about got the capital to launch ourselves, and I believe we've got the will. It'd be crazy not to go for it. *So, what d'you think?*'

Mad Dog didn't stay for the fall-out. He slipped from the room without anybody noticing, and went up to his bedroom. Here, not quite knowing what he was doing, or why, he built an enormous barricade of furniture around his bed and sat behind it in the darkness, wondering what had hit him.

Downstairs, the London people were exploding with fury, Uncle was in a state of shock, villagers were gasping and builders were rubbing their hands with glee at all the new work that would need to be done.

But, upstairs, all Mad Dog could think was that he'd been deceived. For a whole year now, Aunty had been talking about selling the house. Every time Mad Dog had moaned on about how much he hated Devil's Bridge she'd said, 'Not much longer now.'

And he'd believed her. In good faith he'd even helped her. And now the poisoned chalice had been passed on, and it was his. The house loomed over him. The months ahead looked bleak. Who could blame him if he felt conned?

12

Testing the Water

Aunty didn't seem to realise that she was conning anybody. Next day when she tried talking to Mad Dog, she used that phrase again. *Testing the water.* That was all she was doing, she said. Trying something out because she'd always regret it if she didn't.

But Mad Dog wasn't listening. As far as he was concerned, having an inheritance had plainly gone to Aunty's head. Her sisters were right when they whispered behind her back. She *was* a sly one, like they said.

It was the start of a wretched period in Mad Dog's life. The family moved back down to No. 3 but Aunty was scarcely ever there, too busy at Devil's Bridge for any life at home. She tried persuading Mad Dog to join her at weekends, but he was having none of it. What he needed, she said, was a spirit of adventure. But Mad Dog couldn't see anything remotely adventurous about turning his back on the Gap, the barge den, the harbour and the wild waters of the Rheidol in order to move up to some cretinous hotel. Adventures were all to do with waves as high as skyscrapers, wide horizons and open roads. They weren't to do with business undertakings, preparations for Christmas openings and months of organising yet more builders.

Mad Dog hated change, but refused to talk about it. He took to building barricades in his bedroom and hid behind them, trying to keep out of everybody's way.

Aunty hated his barricades because they told her, without a word being said, exactly what he felt about what she was doing. But, for all her dismantling them, Mad Dog was always building new ones and she was never around long enough to stop him.

In this manner, autumn turned to winter and Christmas approached. Aunty was up at the hotel more than she was at home and Uncle started going up there too, taking Elvis with him but leaving Mad Dog round at Luke, Hippie or Rhys's houses, where he was forced to listen to their mothers going on about what a mistake their sister was making.

As far as Christmas was concerned, Mad Dog reckoned it had been cancelled for the year. Maybe there was seasonal cheer along the rest of the Gap, but no one round at No. 3 was putting up decorations, not even a tree, and there was none of the usual smell of Christmas cooking.

Aunty was so busy up at the hotel that she didn't even have time to attend the school carol service in the big town church. And, on the last day of term, it was Uncle who collected Mad Dog outside the school gate, ready to drive him up to Devil's Bridge.

Elvis was in the car already. Its boot was packed with presents, but they made no difference to how Mad Dog felt. As they nosed into the traffic, he saw his friends watching. When they saw that he'd noticed them, they waved. But he didn't wave back.

Mad Dog was in a mood all the way up to the hotel. Santa and a sky full of reindeer couldn't have cheered him up. Neither could the smattering of snow they encountered on the way, dusting hilltops with white flakes.

They drove down through Devil's Bridge, passed the big hotel by the waterfall, looped the hairpin loops and pulled into a second hotel, which Mad Dog couldn't remember ever having seen before, which was surprising because it looked twice as friendly as the one down the road. It took him a moment to realise that they had arrived. Not until Uncle switched off the engine and opened the door, did he get it.

'What do you think?' Uncle said.

Mad Dog eyed the hotel cautiously, unwilling to admit even to himself that it was better than he'd expected. The hotel was bigger and brighter. It seemed solid and alive. Lights blazed at every window and a floodlight illumination announced its new name, THE FALLS HOTEL. A Christmas tree stood outside the front door, hung with coloured lights and Mad Dog could see another one in the entrance hall, along with holly and ivy, glittering glass decorations, pine cones, swathes of ribbon and tall golden candles.

To say that Aunty had transformed the place was an understatement. It wasn't just that she'd turned the crumbling B & B into a proper hotel. She'd brought it to life, and its life was her own. Even sitting in the car, Mad Dog could feel her personality reaching out to greet him.

As if on cue, Aunty came out in person, a smile on her face. She led them indoors to the tree in the reception hall, where their presents were piled up. Mad Dog smelt Christmas cooking coming from the kitchen. He looked around and everywhere were rooms that he didn't remember being there before, but they must have been – it was just that they looked different now. A lounge with books and magazines. A brand new dining room. A bar that shone with glasses and rows of bottles. A little 'snug' where a fire was burning.

'What do you think?' said Aunty.

Mad Dog didn't answer – not because he didn't want to but because he couldn't find the words. Uncle, on the other hand, hugged Aunty hard and said, 'It's a miracle, that's what I think,' and Elvis ran around, wanting Christmas now, and to open all his presents.

Aunty showed him the chimney that had been swept, she said, for Santa to come down. Even Santa had been thought of! After that, Mad Dog couldn't help but soften slightly. Elvis grabbed him and he swirled him round. Then Uncle grabbed them all in his big arms, and he allowed himself to be hugged.

Next day the guests arrived, never knowing that the brightly lit hotel that greeted them had ever been some terrible old B & B. Entirely in her element, Aunty booked them in, took orders for dinner through to the kitchen ladies, Ruth and Kathleen, who were already becoming her replacement sisters, and showed her guests to their rooms. The bar buzzed with voices. The restaurant stood in readiness like a Christmas cake awaiting the first cut. The kitchen clanged with sizzling, steaming pots and pans. The whole house felt *alive*.

Aunty claimed that she was nervous, but it didn't show. She came across as the life and soul of the party, and so did Uncle, doing twenty things at the same time and making every one of them seem easy. It was as if they had been born to run a hotel. Somehow – by accident maybe – it was as if they'd stumbled upon their secret selves. From the moment the first guest arrived, they simply lit up.

It was a better Christmas than any of them had expected, especially Mad Dog, even in his wildest dreams. On Boxing Day, he awoke to find that the smattering of flakes he'd seen on the hills the day they'd arrived had turned into a full-blown Christmas card scenario. After lunch, Uncle organised a trek up the valley as far as the church at Parson's Bridge, whose outer wall was constructed around a series of ancient standing stones. On the way, he and Mad Dog had a little chat about the future. Uncle wanted Mad Dog to know that whatever happened next he and Aunty would never give up No. 3.

'This is *business*,' he said. 'But No. 3's our *home*. I know you've had some worries but I hope you realise that.'

Mad Dog relaxed and allowed himself to enjoy the walk. But perhaps that was a mistake. Perhaps, if he'd been a bit more careful, he'd have noticed that the snow on the road was freezing over, and have trod more carefully, and then his leg wouldn't have shot out from under him and he wouldn't have broken it.

Mad Dog tried to right himself, but that only made things worse. He fell badly and pain shot through him. Everybody crowded round offering hands to help, but he couldn't get up.

'Anyone with a mobile?' the cry went up. 'Who's got reception?' 'Should we phone for an ambulance?'

In the end, Aunty's Range Rover came up from the hotel and Mad Dog was taken down to Aberystwyth where he spent the rest of the day in A & E. It was midnight before he got back, x-rayed and plastered, with instructions to try – for the next few days at least – to keep his foot higher than his head.

From then onwards, Mad Dog was spoiled rotten by family and guests alike. Lying on a sofa in the lounge like a young prince, he only had to ask if he wanted anything. Books, games, chocolates – they were all his. Uncle even drove down to No. 3 and came back with his *ffon*, thinking he might find it easier to manoeuvre himself with than the unwieldy crutches the hospital had supplied.

It proved to be utterly useless in the circumstances, but Mad Dog was strangely pleased to see the old thing again. There was something comforting about the *ffon* that he'd almost forgotten about. Finding it again was like coming across an old teddy bear. It didn't help much in the manoeuvring stakes, but he took to sleeping with it in his arms. He'd long since grown out of hoping for secret messages, but he still ran his fingers over the letters on the silver topknot, spelling them out without even knowing that he was doing it.

One night, awakening from dreams of strange words that made no sense, he turned on the light to look at the word beneath his fingers. WAOOC was what the topknot said. W – A – O – O – C, just one little word, five letters long, but engraved in silver swirls with stars and flowers all round it, and suns and moons and planets.

What did it mean? Mad Dog twisted the cane to see the word more clearly and something rose up in him, like a song. He mightn't have come across this word before, but something about it made his heart want to burst.

Mad Dog closed his eyes. His leg ached beneath the plaster. The night ahead of him had a long way to go and he knew he'd toss and turn throughout it and wake up in the morning feeling tired and grumpy. But, just for now, the world felt sweet because a secret lay within his grasp, waiting to be found out.

13

Aunty's Promise

Returning to the Gap after all the dramas of Christmas at the Falls Hotel was an unexpectedly flat experience. To begin with Mad Dog was the centre of attention, but it wasn't long after his friends had written on his plaster that they started forgetting him. They'd go down to the barge den without wondering if there was any way they could get him there too. Or go out to play football and never even ask if he wanted to come and watch. Just because he couldn't walk properly, they assumed he wouldn't be interested.

It was the same at school. Mad Dog was sure that people didn't mean to leave him out of things, but that was what happened. He was an invisible person, forgotten by everybody in their rush to get on with their busy lives. He took to spending his breaks and lunchtimes in the library, researching the word 'WAOOC' on the internet. Nothing came up, and it still made no sense. It just felt like a jumble of letters.

The weeks seemed endless, dragging on and on. 'When can I have my plaster off?' Mad Dog would ask on an almost daily basis.

'In six weeks' time,' Aunty said to begin with. Then, 'In five weeks' time,' then, 'In three,' then, 'You know when you can have it off. For God's sake stop complaining. You're nearly there. You know you are!'

By now Aunty'd done her sums, knew that Christmas had been a success and was planning to test the water again over the Easter holidays, with a couple of winter weekend-breaks in between. Because of this, the chill was definitely back in the air as far as the sisters were concerned.

'So you're off again, are you?' they said, as half her kitchen disappeared up to the one at Devil's Bridge. 'You want to be careful – soon you'll have nothing left down here.'

Mad Dog worried that they were right. As Easter approached, No. 3 looked less and less like home. Not that Aunty seemed to notice. And Uncle seemed perfectly happy with the way things were, and Elvis plainly couldn't *wait* to get back to the Falls Hotel where he'd been spoiled rotten by all the guests.

Mad Dog's plaster was off by now, which gave him less spare time for brooding. But even so he must have been worrying because, the night before they moved up to the hotel for the Easter fortnight break, he had one of those nightmares that he used to have when he was a little boy, first living at No. 3.

The only difference this time was that it was set in Devil's Bridge, and the Manager was in it, and so were his dogs. They came streaming through the woods, driving everything before them into the rushing waters beneath the waterfall. Mad Dog tried to get away, but they caught his scent and started after him. They chased him up the steep sides of the gorge, tearing through the trees until the Falls Hotel appeared ahead.

For a wonderful moment, Mad Dog thought that he was safe. He tore towards the hotel, only to realise at the last moment that it had turned back into the Aged Relative's B & B. But he headed for it anyway, dashing through the porch and catching a whiff of boiled cabbage again, strong enough to gag him.

But it wasn't the Manager he found waiting for him this time. It was his parents.

Mad Dog's parents. They stood before him, holding out their hands, just the way they'd done in the old dreams he used to have. Mad Dog woke up in a panic, shouting in the darkness and punching the air. Aunty came running. She was at his bedside within seconds.

'What's the matter?' she said.

But Mad Dog couldn't tell her. He couldn't put the bits of dream together. Couldn't work out what they meant. All he could manage was, '*I don't want to go.*'

'Go where?' Aunty said.

'Up to Devil's Bridge,' Mad Dog said. 'I had a dream ... dogs in it ... a chase ... the Manager ...'

'The Manager's gone,' Aunty said. 'There's no way, ever, that I'd let him back. You're safe from him, I promise you.'

But Mad Dog didn't feel safe. At a stroke, his memories of a happy Christmas up at Devil's Bridge were completely wiped away.

'I won't go,' he said. 'You can't make me. I won't. *I won't.*'

Aunty didn't argue. He'd be fine once he got there, she told herself. Just like at Christmas, he'd come round. All the way through Easter, she made sure to keep an eye on him, treating him with care as if he was a special guest. And in every other way things went well. Uncle and Elvis were in their element. The guests loved the place. The weather was great. Even Ruth and Kathleen in the kitchen were great, pulling together in a real team effort that had feasts on the table every night and smiles on every face.

The day the last guest left, Aunty made another of her snap decisions. They were packing up for home and the start of the new school term, and she suddenly announced that, in her opinion, they should bring up everything they needed from No. 3, and spend the rest of the summer at the Falls Hotel. Uncle could carry on with his job in the harbour office, and help in the hotel on evenings and at weekends. And Mad Dog and Elvis – who had just started the reception class – could commute up and down with him on a daily basis, staying with her sisters after school until he could collect them from work.

'But what about No. 3?' Mad Dog said.

'What about No. 3?' Aunty said. 'No. 3's our home, and it always will be. When we've got ourselves on our feet and can afford to employ more staff, we'll move back down. But first we've got to get ourselves established.'

Mad Dog looked at Uncle in the hope that he'd object. But Uncle said that it was the obvious way forward. Mad Dog looked at Elvis. But Elvis – the traitor – was smiling as if Devil's Bridge meant more to him than the Gap had ever done.

Mad Dog swallowed hard. Why did he feel as if everything that had ever been a home to him was slipping away? 'Do you promise, on your word of honour, that if we stay for the summer, we'll go back down to No. 3 in the autumn?' he said.

'As soon as the summer season's over. On our word of honour,' Aunty said.

14

One River

Three days later Uncle hired a van and filled it with their belongings, leaving very little behind. By the time he'd finished, No. 3 looked utterly abandoned, no matter what anybody said about it still being home. On the evening before they moved out, Mad Dog went and sat at the end of the Gap, watching the Rheidol flowing through the harbour. Swans went gliding past him and a heron flew overhead. He watched the river glinting in the fading light and wondered if it would ever be the river of his home again.

Next day they left. Uncle drove the van, and Aunty followed in her Range Rover, which was packed right up to the window of the back door. Everybody lined the Gap and waved them off as if they were royalty. They might only be going for the next few months – and might be making the world's worst mistake, as far as some people were concerned – but leaving the Gap still required a good send-off.

'Really!' Aunty said, as she edged the Range Rover out on to the road. 'It's not as if we're never coming back. You'd think we were emigrating to Australia.'

Maybe they weren't, but it felt like that to Mad Dog. All the way up the Gap, he kept turning back, wanting to be a little boy again, playing on the barge den and kicking balls about on the grass. No. 3 disappeared and he felt a lump in his throat. Then the family disappeared. Then he couldn't see the Rheidol any more, twisting like a piece of spangled silk beyond the walls of the Gap. Then finally the sea disappeared – the great, vast, shifting, shimmering ocean itself, that had brought him those sailors with their stories of adventure.

Mad Dog closed his eyes. Those magic days were gone, just like the sailors had gone and that mermaid long before them. When he opened his eyes again, the whole of Aberystwyth had gone too, with its network of streets, shops and houses that he knew like the back of his hand. He told himself it didn't matter, because he'd be back at school on Monday. But he knew it wouldn't be the same. On Monday morning, the town would be just any town, not the one he lived in. And the Gap would be just any street with houses on it, overlooking some harbour that wasn't special any more because it wasn't home.

The drive up to Devil's Bridge was conducted in silence. Even Elvis sat quietly, as if he knew that something of significance was taking place. He tried holding Mad Dog's hand, as if looking for reassurance. But Mad Dog hadn't forgiven him yet for his betrayal, and wouldn't let him.

They drove over hills, across open moorland, through woodlands and finally into Devil's Bridge, twisting and turning up its hairpin bends until they pulled up outside the Falls Hotel. Here Uncle was waiting for them, having got there first and parked the van. He didn't look very happy.

'I've got one question for you,' he said, as soon as Aunty had parked the Range Rover and jumped out. 'What's *that*?'

He pointed behind the hotel to where, between the kitchen and the dripping cliff, an old battered-looking caravan had been installed.

Aunty braced herself for trouble. 'It's a period piece,' she said.

'*Who's* period piece?' Uncle said.

'It's *our* period piece,' Aunty said. 'I got it cheap on eBay. It's a real bargain. An old 1950s showman's vardo. That's what they used to call them. I bought it as an investment. I thought that we could do it up. Besides, I reckoned that it would solve the accommodation problem.'

'*What* accommodation problem?' Uncle said, a hint of danger in his voice.

Aunty flushed. 'It's like this,' she said. 'We're the victims of our own success. Every available room in the hotel has suddenly been filled, and I've had to book our own rooms too. So what else could I do?'

'You could have told me.'

'I didn't want to bother you.'

Uncle shot Aunty a look that said *lame excuse*. He was no happier with the vardo when he got inside. Elvis wasn't very happy either, complaining that it smelt of old people, whatever that meant.

But Mad Dog felt at home from the word go. Outside the vardo might look run down, but inside it reminded him of the old home he'd lived in before No. 3. It made him feel safe. It was like a nest. It was tiny but everything was there – a fitted kitchen with a bottled-gas stove, a sitting room with an open fireplace, bedrooms with narrow bunk-beds, and a tiny bathroom with a peppermint-coloured sit-up bath.

That evening, with Elvis gone to bed and Aunty and

Uncle busy in the hotel moving furniture about, Mad Dog sneaked off on his own. He needed time to think and take in what was happening. The vardo had changed everything. It wasn't just that he'd found a place where he felt safe, but he'd found a place that stirred old memories.

Mad Dog walked down through the wood, careful to keep to the tourist paths so that he wouldn't get lost. No one else was down there, only him. Trees rose around him, growing precariously out of the steep slopes of a deep gorge.

Mad Dog reached the valley floor, and found a river running through it. Without stopping to think, he peeled out of his trainers and waded straight in. The river was as cold as ice – far colder than the sea – but he didn't flinch, just stood there with it slapping over his ankles, looking up at the sunlit tops of the trees, the light fading fast and the moon rising in a pale, clear sky.

This was all right, he told himself. This river mightn't be the Rheidol, but it would do.

Occasionally Mad Dog heard a car coming along the road above him, its sound fading as it hit the bends, and its headlights disappearing. Then a kingfisher appeared from upriver and flitted past him. A silver fish leapt up, twisting in the air, and the kingfisher dived for it, quickly come and quickly gone in a flash of gold and turquoise.

Finally Mad Dog trailed back up through the wood, listening to blackbirds all the way, singing in the dark. Aunty was cross when he got back, because he'd gone off without saying. But it had been worth it, Mad Dog reckoned. And, besides, if Aunty was going to be so busy all the time, what else could she expect?

From that time on, however, busyness was Aunty's distinguishing characteristic. It was Uncle's too, trying to run two jobs and commute between them. For all their efforts to include him, Mad Dog found himself left on his own. Elvis was fine because he'd made friends in the village. But, when Mad Dog was invited to go and play, he held himself aloof.

Increasingly he felt as if he didn't know where he belonged any more. The hotel pulled one way and No. 3 pulled the other and, between them, Mad Dog didn't know where was home. Every morning at six his day would begin with Aunty's alarm going off and him, Elvis and Uncle leaving the vardo as if it was a mother ship, and driving light years away to the forbidden planet that was life back in Aberystwyth. Then, at the end of the school day, Uncle would pick them up and drive them back to Devil's Bridge, by which time school felt like the mother ship, and the Falls Hotel the next worst thing to oblivion.

Mad Dog felt totally bewildered by it all. Was his true home in the vardo, where he felt safe? Or by the river, which had come to feel like a friend? Or was there no real home for a boy like him? Was he born to be a rover, like his mother had once said?

Mad Dog didn't like thinking about his mother. Whenever he did, darkness closed around him, terrible and deep, just the way it used to do when he'd first lived at No. 3. He started getting snappy and couldn't explain why. There were arguments in the kitchen with Ruth and Kathleen. Arguments with passing guests who, according to Mad Dog, seemed to think he was their servant. One day there was even an argument with Elvis that ended up in a fight.

It started over names. The two of them were on their own in the vardo and Mad Dog decided the time had come to put Elvis straight about this Ryan person that his brother was always calling him.

'My name's not Ryan,' he said tetchily. 'I'm sick of Ryan – stop calling me it!'

'What am I meant to call you, then?' Elvis said.

'You can call me Mad Dog Moonlight,' Mad Dog said.

Elvis burst out laughing. 'That's a *stupid* name,' he said.

Mad Dog turned bright red. 'If you say that again, I'll smash your face in!' he said. 'Besides, your name's not Eric Lewis. It's Elvis Preseli.'

'Don't be stupid – of course it's not!'

'Who are you calling stupid?'

'I'm calling you, Ryan, Ryan, Ryan Lewis –'

'*That's not my name. I TOLD YOU!!*'

Elvis ran around in circles, chanting 'Ryan Lewis' over and over again. It ended up with fists. Mad Dog was twice his brother's size but he didn't even attempt to stop himself. Uncle came in and broke them up. Elvis was giving as good as he got, but Mad Dog was to blame and afterwards he was ashamed of himself.

What was happening to him and Elvis, he wondered later, down by the river where he'd gone to lick his wounds. Once his brother had looked up to him. They'd done everything together, two peas in a pod, one little, one big but the same dark look, the same dark eyes, even the same taste in food and the same love of stories.

Now, however, there was a distance between them. He and Elvis were growing apart. Once he'd been his brother's keeper but now they were scarcely even friends.

Next time he had any spare pocket money, Mad Dog went down to the post office to try and put things right. He bought Elvis a fridge magnet shaped like a Welsh dragon, a bag of sweets, a plastic car and a couple of comics. Then, whilst paying for it all, his eyes fell on a stack of postcards next to the counter. Some were of the waterfalls and bridges that made Devil's Bridge famous, but one was of the gorge with the river flowing through it.

Mad Dog picked up the card to take a closer look. 'I see you like our Rheidolin,' said the woman behind the counter, who had the sort of eyes that never missed anything.

'Your what?' Mad Dog said.

'Our River Rheidol,' the woman said. 'The youngest of Plynlimon's three great rivers – you *do* know what I'm talking about?'

Mad Dog shook his head. 'Are you saying that the river down there in the valley is the *Rheidol*?' he said.

The woman smiled as if the thing was obvious. 'There's only one Rheidolin,' she said.

Mad Dog bought the card along with all the other presents for his brother. On its back he wrote him an apology. He knew that Elvis wasn't old enough to read, and his writing wasn't that good anyway, but he wrote it anyway, then turned it over and stood staring at the river in the picture, marvelling that some things in life hadn't changed, despite what he felt. Only one story flowed through his life, however many different homes he had. One story, and one river, which held it all together. Here in Devil's Bridge and down at No. 3, it was one and the same life. And, whatever name he was called by, he was still the same boy.

Part III
Plynlimon

15

The End-of-Year Project

The discovery about the Rheidol was a major turnabout in Mad Dog's summer. Knowing that the river he'd seen every day down at No. 3 was the same one that flowed through Devil's Bridge changed his attitude to everything. It was crazy to let some nightmare spoil things for him, crazy to let homesickness ruin his summer.

Home was something that could happen anywhere, Mad Dog decided. After that, most of his time was spent down by the river. He set up rope swings, built dens, swam and explored.

Even in school, when his class teacher, Mrs Anwen Jones, suggested that they might like to choose their own subject for the annual end-of-year project, the Rheidol was his choice.

Mad Dog electioneered shamelessly on its behalf, but it was quite a fight. A small group of girls, of whom Grendel Griffiths was the leader, were determined that the project should be on dolphins. And, as anyone who knew the girls in question might have expected, they didn't stay quiet about it either.

But Mad Dog called in favours, twisted arms, cajoled, pleaded and finally won the day. The dolphin group protested, but there was no need for the recount that they demanded. The River Rheidol won hands down.

'This is the last piece of work you'll ever do in this

school,' Mrs Anwen Jones said. 'So come on, class. Show us all what you're made of.'

She sent them off to the library to research the subject of rivers in general and the Rheidol in particular. Soon a map of the entire Rheidol region dominated the classroom, tracing the river all the way from source – or *ffynnon*, as Mrs Anwen Jones called it – to sea. All the birds and animals that lived on and around the river were included on the map, along with villages, bridges, lakes, waterfalls, mountain ranges, roads, railway tracks, old mines, old caves, hydro-electricity generating stations, farms, reservoirs and even the sites of a few long-forgotten castles.

Mad Dog was in his element, learning things about the river that he'd never known before. One day, investigating the possibility of otters down beneath the Devil's Bridge, he came across the post office woman out walking her dog. She knew what he was doing, she said, because her niece was in Mad Dog's class and her friends had voted for the dolphins, but her niece'd stuck her neck out and gone for the Rheidol.

'She made the right choice,' Mad Dog said, marvelling at the way the post office woman always knew everybody's business.

'Of course she did,' the woman agreed. 'The Rheidol's a magical river, but then I'm sure you know that anyway. You spend enough time down here – I'm always seeing you. And when I say magic, I mean *magic*.'

She looked at Mad Dog as if she knew a thing or two. A thrill ran through him. After that, he started researching Rheidol magic on the internet. Sure enough, he found out about all sorts of strange things that didn't get mentioned by Mrs Anwen Jones in class. Bogeys, elves and fairy folk. Black corph candles that heralded death. Characters of dark mystery, like the Red Judge of Plynlimon, who 'came after' children if they were naughty and, according to legend, set his dogs on them – the mythical *cŵn y wbir* or 'Dogs of the Sky'.

But Mrs Anwen Jones wasn't interested in old legends and things like that. 'If you want to research *make-believe*,' she said, 'you're more than welcome. But not in school. What we're looking for here are *hard facts*. The Rheidol may have all sorts of *little stories* associated with it, but if they can't be *researched scientifically* there's no place for them in our class project.'

As if to give an example of the sort of research she called 'scientific', Mrs Anwen Jones arranged for a class visit to the local power station to see how electricity was made. Compared to elves and fairy folk, it didn't sound much fun, but at least it meant a day off school. Letters were sent home with consent forms to be signed, and instructions were issued about what not to wear and how much pocket money to bring.

When the day of the trip arrived, Mad Dog sat on the school bus, braced for a day's worth of total boredom. The last thing he wanted to do was waste a day staring at massive cooling towers and smoking chimneys.

When he arrived, however, there wasn't a chimney in sight. The bus followed the Rheidol to the point where it opened out into a silvery lagoon, then passed through a half-hidden gateway and started up a tree-lined drive. Mrs Anwen Jones rose to her feet and started gathering her belongings together as if they'd arrived somewhere.

'Don't all rush at once,' she said.

The bus drew up in front of a stone building. Mrs Anwen Jones started handing out clipboards and questionnaires, and moving everybody down the aisle. Outside a guide stood waiting to welcome them. The stone building was the power station, she said, and she was here to show them how the waters of the Rheidol could be used to generate electricity. There were no chimneys or cooling towers, just a collection of interconnected reservoirs, dams, aqueducts and hidden pipelines, bringing water down from Plynlimon Mountain, where the Rheidol had its source.

Their guide led them through a computer room full of massive consoles to a cathedral-high chamber housing generators that only required the Rheidol to kick them into life. Down in the bowels of the building, Mad Dog saw the place where it came pouring in, driving the generators to make the electricity. Then, back outside again, he saw the tree-lined cliff where the water came tumbling down from the hills, with a series of man-made pools beneath it, stocked with trout which were being bred to put back into the river.

The day ended with a walk round the lagoon, which was where the water ended up after the generators had finished with it. Mad Dog watched the Rheidol flowing through it on its way down to Aberystwyth. The sky had turned dark above them and someone in the stone building had made the decision to switch on the floodlights, making the lagoon twinkle like something out of fairyland.

At the end of the day, Mad Dog drove back to school with an entirely new impression of the Rheidol. This wasn't just a river for swinging over and making dens. This river worked. It had a job to do. It had a purpose and a use and, every time from this day forward, when a light was switched on or a toaster popped, Mad Dog would think of the river making it happen.

Here on the Rheidol, he thought, even science can be magical.

16

Up Plynlimon

After that, Mad Dog worked like crazy on his project. The hand-in date approached and he printed up everything he could find on every subject from hydro-electricity to Owain Glyndwr, the great Welsh hero who'd unfurled his banner at Glyn Hyddgen, high on Plynlimon, close to the source of the Rheidol, and, in the words of Shakespeare, beaten the English by calling forth 'spirits from the vasty deep'.

His friends were stunned by all the information he dug up, not to say anything of all the time he spent in the school library, and Mrs Anwen Jones praised him for his dedication. When he'd finished, Uncle helped him bind his project and Aunty read it through and pronounced it to be brilliant.

On the morning of the hand-in, five minutes before Uncle was due to drive them down to Aberystwyth, Mad Dog Google-Earthed a map of the Rheidol's *ffynnon* to use as its cover. It was amazing to see the river coming into focus, clicking down from Planet Earth to Europe, to the British Isles, to Wales and eventually to Plynlimon Mountain.

Mad Dog stared at the mountain, taking in all its contours, all its dips and ridges and valleys. The three great rivers that the post office woman had told him about were plain to see, and there in between them was the *ffynnon* of the Rheidol – a small black lake called Llyn Rheidol, marked in English as 'Eye of the Rheidol'.

Mad Dog found it impossible to stop staring at it. If it hadn't been for Uncle shouting for him to hurry up, he'd have been late for school. When Mrs Anwen Jones saw the size of the project that he hauled in, she said he should feel proud. But, once he'd handed it over, all he felt was horribly flat. It was as if something important had passed out of his life. There was nothing to get excited about any more. Nothing to work towards or look forward to, except the end of term followed by a new school in the autumn – and that was something Mad Dog didn't know whether to wish for or dread. Even when Mrs Anwen Jones announced that, as a reward for all their hard work, she was taking the class up to Llyn Rheidol, to see for themselves the river's source, it didn't have the power to cheer him up.

Everybody else was excited, even those who didn't like the countryside and hated walking, because it meant a day out of the classroom. But Mad Dog was in such a bad mood that he didn't even bother telling Aunty, and she only discovered the night before. Then there was a panic to find the things on Mrs Anwen Jones's equipment list, including a suitable knapsack for carrying provisions and shoes strong enough for walking over difficult terrain.

It was the shoes that Mrs Anwen Jones made the biggest fuss about, oddly enough. The day before the trip she made a speech about them, listing the different types of shoe and boot that would and wouldn't do, and particularly saying no fashion items please.

'And make sure you bring drinks and sunhats too,' she added. 'And waterproofs, just in case of rain. Plynlimon's not a mountain to be played around with.

It's unpredictable and full of surprises. It mightn't look much from a distance, but the closer you approach it, the bigger it gets. People have been known to get into trouble up there, partly because they underestimate the size of it and partly because they don't listen to the weather forecast before they set out. But we'll be all right. Don't you worry. The weather forecast's good, and you're all going to bring the right shoes, *aren't you*?'

Next day, however, the sky was cloudy. Against all expectations, clouds came blowing in from the sea, and the handful of parents and dinner ladies who'd volunteered as helpers looked as though they wondered what they were in for. So did the class, especially the Grendel gang, and the situation wasn't made any better when word came through that Mrs Anwen Jones, out celebrating her first wedding anniversary the night before, had been crippled by a bout of food poisoning – which meant that *Mrs Heligan* was in charge instead!

When he heard that, Mad Dog felt like walking out. He'd never forgotten how miserable Mrs Heligan had made him in his first year at school. And nothing about her had changed, it seemed. She came marching into the classroom, lined them up, helpers and all, and made a speech about being good, as if they were all still five.

'If it wasn't for me, this trip would have been called off,' she said. 'So I'm expecting you to behave yourselves, and *work hard*.'

The idea that the day was meant to be a treat seemed not to have occurred to her. Before they set off, she divided the class into pairs that had nothing to do with personal friendships and everything to do with the fact that girls, in her view, were plainly more sensible than boys.

Mad Dog ended up sitting on the bus next to Grendel Griffiths, which couldn't have been a worse pairing for either of them. Grendel tried changing seats, but Mrs Heligan hauled her back. Then she complained that Mad Dog had hit her, but all Mrs Heligan did was fix Mad Dog with her stony eyes and say, 'Nothing much has changed with you, has it? *Watch it, Ryan!*'

Poor old Grendel – she even tried wheezing, on the principle that she was allergic to Mad Dog. But Mrs Heligan told her to pull herself together and stop being stupid.

'My dad'll get you if you talk to me like that,' said Grendel.

'I'd like to see him try it,' Mrs Heligan replied.

All the way up to Plynlimon, Mad Dog and Grendel sat looking in opposite directions, making sure their eyes didn't meet. Grendel played games on her mobile phone and Mad Dog looked out of the window and clutched his *ffon*. Why he'd brought it with him, he didn't know. Everyone had laughed when he'd turned up with it, especially Rhys and Hippie, who'd said that walking sticks were for old women. But, when Mad Dog had woken up that morning, the *ffon* had been the first thing he'd seen – there by his bed, waiting to be picked up.

At the village of Ponterwyd, the school bus turned off the main pass road and started up a smaller one, signposted to the Nant y Moch reservoir. The view ahead was glorious – rolling mountains and open grasslands, grazing pastures and wide skies. It should have raised even Mad Dog's spirits, but it was hard to feel cheerful with Mrs Heligan sitting right behind him.

Only when the reservoir itself came into view – a great expanse of sapphire-blue water held back by a massive dam – did Mad Dog start to cheer up. The view ahead of him was astonishing. Mountains ringed the lake with not a tree or shrub in sight – great golden mountains crowned with grasslands that looked as yellow as sunlight despite the grey clouds overhead.

At the sight of them, Mad Dog started feeling as if this trip just might be all right, Grendel or no Grendel. The school bus eased itself over a cattle grid, then took a winding road that led down to the lakeside. Here it ended up in a stony little lay-by with nothing around for miles but the waters of Nant y Moch and a huge, sweeping valley surrounded by hills.

Mrs Heligan stood up and announced the obvious. 'We've arrived.'

Everybody tumbled off the bus, eager to explore, only to find themselves buffeted by strong winds that tugged at bodies and whipped hair across faces. For a moment all pairings were forgotten as they struggled into waterproofs and heaved on knapsacks. Mrs Heligan clapped her hands and called them all to order. She lined them up in their designated twosomes to be ticked off on a clipboard and handed out maps, information sheets and questionnaires that had been prepared for them by Mrs Anwen Jones, never intending them to be instruments of torture – but that was what they were now!

'You might have finished working on your projects,'

Mrs Heligan announced. 'But that doesn't mean that you can't learn more. I shall test how much you've discovered when we stop for lunch. And again when we get back to school. Mrs Anwen Jones would expect nothing less from me. I expect all your questionnaires to be completed by the end of the day. And no sections left out, if you please. Oh, and tidy handwriting, of course, and *mind your spelling*.'

Everybody shivered and started heading for the track that wound up the valley, parallel to the lake. But again Mrs Heligan clapped her hands. She hadn't finished with them yet.

'I expect you to keep your eyes on each other, and not go astray,' she called after them. 'You've been put in pairs to take responsibility for each other. So mind where you go and what you do. And keep your waterproofs close to hand because there may be rain. And your sunhats, in case the weather changes – although it doesn't look very likely. And Ryan Lewis, that walking stick of yours is for *walking*, not *sword fighting*. If I catch you doing anything else with it, it's detention for the rest of the week.'

There were sniggers all round. Mad Dog brandished his *ffon* and played it for laughs. Grendel rolled her eyes. Luke asked what would happen if the weather turned any worse. But, as if it wouldn't dare – not on her watch – Mrs Heligan ignored the question and dispatched parents and dinner ladies to man the various checkpoints along the track.

The class was to be at checkpoint three by twelve o'clock, she said, prior to walking up Plynlimon together, following the river until they reached Llyn Rheidol near the top. There – and *not* before – they'd eat their packed lunches together, then they'd return to the lake at Nant y Moch at three on the dot, where the bus would be ready to take them back to school.

With a final *make sure you keep your eyes on the time*, Mrs Heligan sent the class off to find the answers on their questionnaires, waving her hands as if they were a cloud of mosquitoes she was trying to get rid of. Grendel tried to join up with her gang, but Mrs Heligan shouted *partners please* at her and she flounced off in a pair of kitten-heeled pink boots that she'd chosen to wear despite everything Mrs Anwen Jones had said.

Mad Dog decided he'd better stick with her – not because he wanted to but because he was aware that Mrs Heligan was watching them with eagle eyes. He flung on his knapsack and started along the track, following the line of the lake. The two of them walked in silence. Rhys was just in front of them, partnering the post office lady's niece whom he had always fancied, which was great for him.

Mad Dog kept turning round, but Mrs Heligan was always right behind, her head down against the wind, her expression sour as if she wished that she, not Mrs Anwen Jones, was the one tucked up in bed nursing food poisoning. They'd only just started walking but she looked fed-up already. Mad Dog couldn't think why she'd volunteered to replace Mrs Anwen Jones. She plainly had no interest in where they were going.

'What happens when we reach the end of this valley?' Rhys asked as the end of the lake came into sight.

'Work it out yourself. You've got a map. Use your eyes. You children are so lazy,' Mrs Heligan snapped.

Mad Dog knew she didn't have the answer. 'We're going up there,' he explained to Rhys, pointing to the biggest crag in sight – Plynlimon Fawr – which rose above them to a lofty height.

'What, *up there*?' said Rhys, looking shocked. 'Are you sure? There must be some mistake.'

Mad Dog grinned. He said there was no mistake. That was where the river was leading them. It was obvious, even without a map.

'I thought this was meant to be a *walk*,' Rhys said.

'Now who's the old woman?' replied Mad Dog.

17

Wilderness

For as long as Mrs Heligan was still behind them, Mad Dog stuck to Grendel like a puppy in training classes. But, as soon as she decided to see what the class was getting up to further along the track, he was off.

'What do you think you're doing?' Grendel called as he left the track and everybody else, and started picking his way down to the place where the Rheidol flowed into the lake.

'I'm doing us both a favour,' he called back.

'You'll get us into trouble.'

'See if I care.'

Grendel stomped off, shouting, 'See if I care,' too.

Mad Dog turned his back on her. When he reached the lake, he skimmed stones across its surface until she'd disappeared from sight. Then he started picking his way upriver, guessing that the track which the rest of the class were walking along ran parallel to him. It was nicer down here than up there with everybody else. The landscape all around him made him feel alive, and his *ffon* was all the company he needed.

Mad Dog walked alone for ages, the wind whipping up the valley and beating him on the back. Only when he remembered about the twelve o'clock checkpoint did he leave the river and cut up the side of the valley, looking for the track. It was a tougher climb than he'd expected, and took longer too. He passed three tracks on the way, and they all looked pretty much the same, but none of them had parents on them, or checkpoints or any sign of classmates.

Mad Dog crossed a fourth track, and finally decided that he was lost. By shaking off Grendel he hadn't intended to shake off the rest of the class, but that was what he'd done. Mad Dog looked around, trying to work out what to do next. Grendel had their map but, reckoning that he could manage without it, he abandoned all thought of following tracks and started straight up Plynlimon Fawr, heading for the Rheidol's source, where they'd be meeting for lunch.

Mrs Heligan was going to be mad at him but, by taking the difficult but direct route, Mad Dog reckoned he ought to be able to get up to Llyn Rheidol ahead of her. He tried phoning Rhys to explain what he was doing but discovered he had no reception. Not that it mattered, he told himself. Rhys and the others would find him soon enough. And, *even* if he did end up in trouble with Mrs Heligan, there was nothing he could do about it now, so he might as well enjoy himself.

'At least I've got no one telling me what to do,' he said out loud. 'No stupid questionnaire to fill in, and no Grendel to argue with. And look what a day it's turned into!'

By now the wind had dropped, the grey clouds had rolled away and the sun had come out. Mad Dog peeled out of his waterproofs and stuffed them into his knapsack. Above his head, the sky was a bright, clear blue, and he remembered what Mrs Anwen Jones had said about Plynlimon being unpredictable. Behind him he could see the reservoir at Nant y Moch, sparkling like a jewel in a ring of golden mountains. All around him, for mile upon mile, there was not a tree or house or road or car or person in sight.

'If I had to get lost anywhere,' Mad Dog reckoned, 'I couldn't have chosen better than this beautiful wilderness.'

Not that he was *really* lost, of course. Mad Dog pressed on up the mountain, eyes fixed on the cliffs of Plynlimon Fawr, which never seemed to get any closer but he couldn't somehow bring himself to care. All around him, turquoise gadflies, bright pink foxgloves, silver cotton-grass and dots of yellow celandines wove a web of bright colour. A red kite wheeled overhead. A strip of bright blue ocean revealed itself on the horizon.

Mad Dog marvelled at it all. He could pick out the Rheidol running round the foot of Plynlimon Fawr, and it *was* a magic river like the post office woman had said. In fact, more than merely magical, this place felt holy. Mad Dog wasn't quite sure what he meant by that, but *holy* felt like the only word big enough to cover it. Almost without his noticing, his pace slowed down. He was still looking for Llyn Rheidol, but getting there before Mrs Heligan no longer seemed important. This climb was his to enjoy. It was meant for savouring. In a place like this, time didn't matter. In fact, in a place like this, no matter how many detours he took there was no such thing as *lost*.

Finally the path levelled out and a string of ponds appeared ahead of Mad Dog like pearls in a necklace, set on a bed of velvety moss. He passed the first pond, which was full of cotton-grass and orange butterflies. Then he passed a second one, covered with yellow lilies and huge green pads. Finally he drew level with the third pond, whose waters looked as clear as cut-glass, and he couldn't resist stooping to drink.

The water had a taste of Aunty's mulled Christmas wine about it, although that was warm and this was ice-cold. Mad Dog watched circles radiating out from his cupped hands and could have stayed for ever, watching them growing and drinking handful after handful of clear crystal water.

But then a red kite wheeled overhead, crying out loud and casting a shadow over him – and Mad Dog looked up and remembered his classmates. He set off again, checking his phone, but still he didn't have reception. He turned back once, and the ponds shone again like pearls, and he could see the blue waters of Nant y Moch below them and, in the distance, he could see the ocean.

After that, the great cliffs of Plynlimon Fawr started closing in and Mad Dog's walk – though not so steep – was cast in shadows. The red kite soared away and silence seeped into Mad Dog. Once streams had run beside him, but not any more. No springs rose out of the ground and the path ahead of him became increasingly stony and rough.

Mad Dog started wondering if he was heading in the right direction. For the first time since heading up Plynlimon Fawr, he began to doubt what he was doing. Surely he'd never find Llyn Rheidol up here. No river could have its source in such a dry and stony place as this.

Mad Dog pressed on all the same, but the cliffs continued to close in around him until it was obvious that anything but turning back was completely crazy.

But still Mad Dog carried on, and suddenly the cliff on one side of him dropped away and he caught a glimpse of water. There it was at last – a sudden, stunning blackness forming a stark contrast to the bright blue sky.

The Eye of the Rheidol!

Mad Dog started running. Cliffs fell behind him on the other side as well, and he came out of the shadows and felt the sun on his face. Suddenly the whole lake was spread out before him. It had grasslands on one side of it, and a rock wall on the other, covered with wild flowers and a network of cobwebs set alight by the sun.

For a moment, the view was so beautiful, opened out before him in the folds of the mountain, that Mad Dog started laughing. He was still laughing when he reached the lake. He couldn't stop. Ignoring a battered old sign that said NO SWIMMING, he tore off his clothes and waded straight in. It was a hot day, but that wasn't why he did it. He did it because something inside him wanted to possess the lake. To even be a part of it. To get up close.

Mad Dog swam across the lake with strong strokes that would have astonished anyone who'd ever seen him swim before, then pottered back at a more recognisable pace. Only when he climbed out did he finally realise that Mrs Heligan and the class had long-since come and gone, leaving flattened grass behind them and a couple of crisp packets.

Mad Dog picked them up. He was really in trouble now, but so what? If the others weren't here, he didn't care. In fact, if they *had* been here, everything would have been spoiled.

Without bothering to put his clothes back on, Mad Dog flung himself down in the long grass to eat his picnic lunch and enjoy the sun on his skin. He should have been worrying about how late it was, but Plynlimon had cast a spell on him and the only thing that mattered was being here.

When he'd finished eating, Mad Dog went searching for what he'd come for in the first place – the *ffynnon* of the Rheidol. He found it at last in the long grass at the top end of the lake, shivering its way out of darkness into daylight. Here he flung himself face-down on a slab of sun-baked rock to watch the little trickle of newborn water starting its long journey down through the lake to Aberystwyth's harbour.

Mad Dog closed his eyes and listened. Suddenly it seemed to him that he had the power to hear the river pass through every place along the way, from Nant y Moch and Devil's Bridge, to the Gap, No. 3 and finally the sea. He pressed his face against the sun-baked rock. Everything else felt small and passing – Grendel, Mrs Heligan, his classmates, even Aunty and Uncle. Here on Plynlimon, he felt caught up in something bigger than himself. He tried to imagine Plynlimon a hundred years ago ... a thousand years ago ... a million ...

Hours later, Mad Dog awoke. By now the slab of rock had cooled down and shadows had fallen, bringing with them a thin veil of evening mist that hung over the lake. Mad Dog shivered, and got up. The sweep of sunlit grassland that surrounded the lake had turned a cool grey and a little bit of night breeze blew his way.

Mad Dog found his clothes and pulled them on.

Then he packed his knapsack and, making sure to leave no litter behind, started heading down the lake. He was in big trouble, wasn't he? By now the school bus would be long-since gone, but there'd be people left behind, he had no doubt. People looking for him – and they were going to be furious when they found him!

Reaching the point where the newly formed Rheidol started its tumbling journey down to Nant y Moch, Mad Dog said goodbye to the lake. The sky was darkening now, and the stars coming out. The valley ahead of him looked thoroughly unwelcoming, and Plynlimon didn't feel holy any more. It felt like an old witch of a mountain that had cast a spell on him. Either that, or a spider of a mountain that had caught him in its web.

Mad Dog started down the valley just as the last light faded and night came in its place. He couldn't see the Rheidol any more and, worse still, it wasn't long before he couldn't hear it either. Somewhere in the darkness it had simply disappeared.

Mad Dog stopped to listen, but the silence created by the absence of the river was overwhelming. It was a silence that changed everything. Even the shape of the valley seemed different without the sound of the Rheidol running through it.

Where had it gone? The river had been his lifeline and, without it to steer by, the mountain around him seemed huge and formless. He set off again, edging his way forward with nothing to steady himself. Not even his *ffon*.

His ffon!

What had happened to his ffon?

In a moment of panic, Mad Dog spun round and

almost lost his balance. At first he thought he must have dropped it on the ground, but it wasn't anywhere that he could see, and he couldn't remember the last time he'd had it either. Had it been at Llyn Rheidol, where he'd slept on that rock? Or by his clothes when he'd gone swimming? Or had he lost it earlier than that – by that crystal pond, say, where he'd stopped to drink? Or, even before that – had he left it down at Nant y Moch?

Mad Dog couldn't remember, but it was too dark to mount a search party now, which meant that he was going to have to spend the night on Plynlimon and start afresh in the morning.

'No way, *no wa*y, am I going home without my *ffon*,' he said.

The idea was unthinkable. But what if he never found it? That idea was even more unthinkable and, cursing himself for having brought it with him in the first place, Mad Dog looked around for a place to spend the night.

At first, however, there was nothing. Mad Dog stumbled down the valley with nothing but vast emptiness around him and darkness pressing in. Not a tree or ruined cottage caught his eye, not a cave or any other place of shelter. Finally, the best he could find was a broken-down old sheep's pen with a low scrub of bushes growing behind it. It wasn't much, but it was better than nothing.

Mad Dog curled up tight in the side of the wall, hoping that it would shelter him if the wind blowing up the valley got any worse. What am I doing here? he thought. This is crazy. How did I ever get myself into this mess?

The grass beneath him was soft and mossy, but the ground beneath that was decidedly damp. Mad Dog shivered, imagining a soft, warm bed and lots of food. It was hours now since he'd eaten, and hours longer, he guessed, before he would again.

Mad Dog dug out his phone to check the time, but found the battery flat. He closed his eyes, exasperated that this too seemed set against him, and started counting off the minutes in his head. Somewhere out there at the end of them was morning. All he had to do was count, and it would finally arrive. He got to three minutes thirty-seven seconds. Three minutes thirty-eight. Three minutes thirty-nine – and then, despite the cold and the damp, exhaustion took him and he was asleep.

18

A Monster on the Mountain

Sometime during the night Mad Dog awoke to find himself under attack. A monster came at him in the darkness, all shrieks and claws. He woke up fighting, trying to shake it off. He wanted to believe that it was only a dream, but the monster was too real for that. It was shaking him awake, yelling at him, clinging to him, shouting in his face.

What was going on? It took Mad Dog moments to grasp that the monster wasn't trying to kill him and wasn't even a monster, anyway. But the realisation brought no comfort.

For the monster was Grendel Griffiths.

Grendel Griffiths! On the mountain. In the night. Lost, like him. Frozen, like him. Scared, like him. *How could this be?*

Before he could work it out, Grendel hit him with a stick – and then flung herself into his arms.

'This is all your fault!' she cried, clinging on tight and refusing to let go. 'I hate you!'

Mad Dog didn't know what was worse, fighting Grendel or being hugged by her. She pinned him with one leg and hit him with the stick, which she clutched in her spare hand. Her breath on his face smelt of chewing gum, and her voice carried on about what she was going to do to him when they returned to civilisation. But, even so, she wouldn't let him go.

Struggling to get her off him, Mad Dog reached for

the stick – only to recognise it.

'My *ffon*!' he cried out. 'That's my *ffon*! Where did you find it?'

He tried even harder to grab the stick, but Grendel clung on tight. She wouldn't say where she'd found it, only that it was hers. The two of them rolled over on the ground, Grendel shrieking, 'Get off me!' and, 'It's mine,' and, 'Find your own stick,' until finally Mad Dog wrenched it out of her grasp.

At this, Grendel started crying that everything that had happened to her was all Mad Dog's fault. She started hitting Mad Dog's chest with her balled-up fists.

'What's my fault?' he demanded to know.

'Everything,' Grendel repeated, 'beginning with Mrs Heligan blaming me for your getting lost. She said that, as my partner, you were my responsibility, and she made me go back and find you.'

'She made you do *what*?' Mad Dog said.

Grendel bawled. 'It was terrible,' she wept. 'First I lost the map, and then the heels came off my boots – both my boots, which means you owe me, by the way, because they were new – and then I don't quite know what happened but every track I took always turned out wrong. And then, finally, it got dark. It was cold and scary, and I couldn't see where I was going, not until I found that stick shining in the long grass. And now you've taken it and its light has gone out.'

Mad Dog didn't know what light she meant, and Grendel was in no mood to explain. 'When I get home, I'm going to set my dad on you,' she said.

Mad Dog shivered at the mention of Grendel's father, who was not a man to be messed with from what he'd heard. Grendel said again that she hated him – but that didn't stop her pressing herself against him on the principle that two bodies were better than one, and he was warmer than nothing.

She was right too. Mad Dog closed his eyes and prayed for dawn. The knack, he discovered, was to try and pretend that Grendel was someone else – his mother, for example, rocking him to sleep, or Aunty, or a nice warm fire. He prayed for morning too, or, at least, for Grendel to fall asleep, but her voice went on and on, covering every subject from sore feet to the recurring threat of what her father would do when Mad Dog came within his grasp.

The only small pleasure Mad Dog could glean from the situation came from imagining what her father might do to Mrs Heligan as well, not to say anything of the school. Hopefully they'd sack her and she'd never teach again. After all, she was the one who'd sent Grendel back.

But she wasn't the one, according to Grendel, who'd end up getting sued. 'Just you wait,' she breathed into Mad Dog's face. 'By the time my dad's finished, you and your family won't have a penny between you!'

Mad Dog tried to sleep, but lay awake for most of the night. When Grendel finally dropped off, he still couldn't sleep, not even when he tried counting. But it wasn't her father he was thinking about, or what would happen when the school found out he'd spent a night alone on a mountain with Grendel Griffiths. It was his *ffon* that occupied his thoughts – the strange way that it did that, come back to him every time he thought he'd lost it. And that thing Grendel had said about the light – what had *that* been all about?

By the time that dawn broke, Mad Dog was worn out with thinking, as stiff as a board and soaked through from lying on the edge of what turned out to be a bog. As soon as it was light enough, he left Grendel snoring like a prize fighter with blocked sinuses and went to work out where they were. Below the sheep's pen, he could make out what looked like a major crossroads between valleys with a river running through it that, he guessed, had a good chance of being the Rheidol. If it was, Mad Dog told himself, and he could find a way down to it, then he and Grendel could be back in civilisation in no time.

Mad Dog set off to investigate. The valley turned out to be easier to get down than he'd expected, but the river was bigger than it appeared from a distance, and too deep to breach. Mad Dog had to cross two other streams before he could even get to it, then wade upriver to a place where it looked shallow enough to pick his way across – except that it wasn't as shallow as it looked, which meant he suddenly found himself up to his waist in water.

Mad Dog clambered out, frozen and gasping, and started running on the spot, trying to keep warm. A small hillock stood on this side of the river and he started up it, hoping to find the waters of the reservoir when he reached the top. Cliffs rose on one side of him and sloping grassland ran down the other to the river. A stony track lay ahead of him and, tucked into its side, lay the ruins of a cottage with collapsed walls and the broken remains of a chimney breast with a blackthorn tree growing out of it.

Mad Dog slowed down when he saw the cottage. It

was the first sign of human habitation he'd come across since yesterday but, instead of warming to it, he found himself going as cold on the inside as he was on the outside.

What was the matter with him? Mad Dog pressed on up the hillock, telling himself that what he felt was nothing to do with the cottage itself, and all to do with having spent a night out in the open. But, as the cottage grew closer, he slowed down until, by the time he was level with it, he'd stopped altogether, feeling physically sick.

'Come on,' he goaded himself. 'You're nearly there. At the top of the hillock, you'll see Nant y Moch. And there are farms beyond Nant y Moch. You could get down to them in an hour. Then you'll get breakfast and a bed, and they'll come and rescue Grendel, and phone Aunty and the school, and everything will be all right.'

Mad Dog tried again, but with no success. It was as if a physical barrier was stopping him from going any further.

Finally, feeling as if monsters of the order of the Red Judge of Plynlimon and his Dogs of the Sky lay on the other side of that hillock, Mad Dog turned back. The crossroads between valleys stretched out before him, with the river flowing through it and the cottage in the centre of his vision. And suddenly it all looked so familiar that Mad Dog cried out. If he'd been standing on the path to No. 3, the view couldn't have looked more familiar.

'I don't understand! *What's going on here?*'

After that, everything became a bit of a blur. Mad Dog started running back down the track as if the

Dogs of the Sky really were after him. He'd no idea where he was going, but somehow he made it back across the river, and found himself at the sheep pen again, where a furious Grendel, thinking that he'd abandoned her, waited for him.

'I was getting worried. Where've you been?' she shrilled at him.

'Nowhere,' Mad Dog cried, trying to extract himself. 'I've been nowhere. Believe me – *it was nowhere*.'

He grabbed his things and tore off. Grendel tore after him. 'Where d'you think you're going?' she shrieked. 'What about me? Hey, wait!'

After that, they ran for hours, getting twice as lost as they'd been before. One valley led to another, one river to another. The ground was rough and the going hard. There were no more ruined cottages or other signs of civilisation. Sometimes they found themselves on open grasslands that seemed to stretch for miles, sometimes running over heather, sometimes wading through peat bogs.

Finally they ended up in forestry commission land on the far side of Plynlimon. Grendel pleaded with Mad Dog to stop, certain that they were running round in circles. But Mad Dog didn't even want to slow down. A shadow had fallen over him when he'd reached that ruined cottage, and it refused to go away. If those legendary Dogs of the Sky – the Red Judge's *cŵn y wbir* – really had been after him, Mad Dog couldn't have felt more frightened. Anything could happen on a mountain like this. *Unpredictable* was the word that Mrs Anwen Jones had used for it. And she hadn't been far wrong.

By now, Mad Dog was so scared that he could

almost see the Red Judge of Plynlimon along with his dogs, stalking through the misty forest with deadly intent. He could almost hear their breath. Almost smell them. They were that real.

Trees shivered as he tore past, and he shivered too and so did Grendel. His panic was a disease, and she had caught it. The two of them ran together, stumbling and falling, tripping and crying.

Not even when a road appeared beneath them did they stop. A road. A proper, tarmac, made-up road! At the sight of it, Grendel's legs almost gave way but Mad Dog pulled her on, yelling at her that she mustn't give up now.

They reached the road, and started racing along it. By now their clothes were torn and their legs scratched and bleeding. A village sign came into view, announcing OLD HALL, but they scarcely noticed it. They passed a group of cottages without stopping. Passed a school, a church and a farm with barns on the road.

They would have carried on too, if someone hadn't stopped them.

'Hey, you two? Where are you going? Are you all right? What are you up to? Stop right there! *Stop, I say!*'

It was Grendel who stopped first. She turned her head and saw an elderly woman heading towards them from the back of a parked car, and a second woman, obviously her sister, straightening up from unpacking bags of shopping.

'Of course they're not all right,' this second woman said, then called to them, 'Don't be scared. We won't bite. Come over here. Let's take a look at you.'

Mad Dog would have dragged Grendel away. His fear had reached such a pitch that he dared not trust anyone, not even a pair of sweet, white-haired old ladies with well-meaning, if slightly bossy, voices.

But Grendel had had enough. It only took a smile on the first woman's face – and she burst into tears and flung herself into her arms.

19

The Ingram Sisters

Mad Dog knew he couldn't leave Grendel on her own. The women sounded well-meaning, but they could be anybody. They started ushering Grendel up a garden path towards a heavy oak front door, and he followed, half-expecting to find a gingerbread cottage inside, with ovens big enough for cooking children. Even when he discovered that the house was a converted chapel rather than a witches' lair, it didn't make any difference to how he felt.

Grendel disappeared inside before he could get her back. He reached the porch and stared at a brass nameplate that said ST CURIG'S HOUSE. INGRAM. NO HAWKERS OR CIRCULARS. GENUINE CALLERS ONLY. The oak door remained open, but Mad Dog stood before it for ages, trying to work out what to do. He knew he should go in, and felt a coward for staying outside. But there was a wilderness inside his head. Wild places. Wild things. Scary thoughts. A world of nameless fears that held him back.

No one tried to make Mad Dog go in, although one of the old ladies did stick her head round the door to check if he was still there. Finally, however, managing to get a grip on himself, he stepped inside to find himself in a large open-plan all-purpose room where there were no ovens, cauldrons or books of spells, only an untidy chaos that spelt out the word *home*. Relief washed over him. But what had happened to Grendel?

The women led him to the bathroom, where he found her wrapped in a massive towel, looking like an ordinary girl again, the terror washed out of her. At the smell of soap and the sight of hot, comforting steam, Mad Dog felt the wilderness drain out of him.

After Grendel had finished in the bathroom, pausing only to examine her face in the mirror, he had a shower too. Then all the scratches on his legs were attended to as if the women were used to rescuing injured people off the mountain. He was put in fresh clothes, which didn't fit but at least felt warm, then he joined Grendel in front of massive plates of eggs, mushrooms, fried tomatoes and honey cakes.

In all this time, the old women didn't ask a single question about what they'd been doing to end up in such a state. But once they'd eaten, they were fair game. The women settled them on a massive sofa before a window which was full of sunlight. Then they wanted to know everything. And some of their questions were very pointed too. Not only did they ask 'Who are you?', 'Where do you come from?' and 'Do your parents know where you are?' but, 'Why were you on Plynlimon?', 'Did something frighten you?' and – most pointedly of all – 'What were you running from?'

The questions came thick and fast, with very little time to answer before the next one came along. Mostly it was the Ingram sister with the glasses who spoke – the one who'd stopped them in the first place, her mouth snapping open and shut like a letterbox. Apart from that, the two of them were fairly interchangeable, both tall and thin with the same twin peaks of old ladies' hair piled up on their heads, and the same bright sisters' eyes that looked from Mad Dog to Grendel as if they knew more about Plynlimon than they were letting on.

Mad Dog tried explaining that they'd been on a school trip and had got lost. But, as if she was afraid of him glossing over the true nature of the situation, Grendel suddenly burst out with, 'I want my dad! You've got to phone him. None of this is any of my fault. He's to blame – him, Ryan Lewis! He did the whole thing just to frighten me! He's a beast. I've always hated him. I hope the school expels him. I hope the police arrest him. And they should too, because right from the start, *he had the whole thing planned!*'

Mad Dog was furious, but there was nothing he could do to stop it. Words like *injustice* and *bare-faced lying* sprang to mind, but Grendel wouldn't let him get a word in edgeways. Finally, when she'd finished her character assassination, she flung herself back on the sofa and concluded with, 'In case you're wondering, I'm Grendel Griffiths and this is my phone number and I want to go home *right now.*'

One of the Ingram sisters phoned Grendel's father – and then all hell broke loose. You'd have thought that Grendel's dad would have been relieved to hear that his princess was safe, but all that came across was anger.

'At least they're alive,' the Ingram sister said down the phone. 'However much they've been through, at least they're off Plynlimon with only a few scratches and bruises to show for it. Some people go up there and never come back. And yet here they are, safe and well.'

When Grendel's dad finally turned up, the last thing

Mad Dog felt was safe and well. He'd never actually spoken to Mr Griffiths before, but he'd seen him around school – a hulk of a man, given to few words, whose redeeming feature was his jewel of a daughter. One of the Ingram sisters went to answer the thundering on the door and, as Grendel's father came storming in, Mad Dog found himself reaching for his *ffon*.

Mr Griffiths had one of those faces that look angry at the best of times, but now it bore all the major features of a bull on a rampage. He came straight at Mad Dog without even stopping to greet Grendel, picked him up by the scruff of his neck, and shouted, '*So you're the boy that everybody's telling me about!*'

Mad Dog whispered that, yes, he was that boy, whereupon Mr Griffiths opened his mouth so wide that Mad Dog could see halfway down his throat, and roared, '*I'm going to kill you, so help me God.*'

He started shaking Mad Dog, and it took the combined effort of Grendel, shouting at him to 'lay off, Dad', and the full force of the Ingram sisters, to get him to stop. They were tough old women too – far stronger than they looked. But, by the time they'd extracted Mad Dog, he felt like a rag doll that had been pulled to pieces.

Grendel's father stood over him, trembling with fury. 'You think you can mess with my daughter?' he roared. 'You think you can mess with me? You think you can mess with my family? Well, we'll see about that! Nobody – *and I mean nobody* – takes my daughter up some mountain and gets her lost!'

Finally he was persuaded to leave, grabbing Grendel on the way and storming out of the house without even thanking the sisters for what they'd done. When his car had roared away, the silence was overwhelming. The sisters made a pot of life-restoring amber tea because, they reckoned, Mad Dog needed it and so did they. Then they led him out into the garden because they reckoned they needed that too. The three of them sat on wrought-iron seats, looking at flowers and bees, drinking like guests at a vicarage tea party while they waited for Uncle to arrive.

It was the first time since setting sight on that ruined cottage that Mad Dog had felt anything approaching a sense of peace. He leant back in the sunshine and hugged his *ffon*. It was good to be here. He savoured the moment. The sisters were chattering about honey and pollen and St Curig's bees, and he could see the bees in question dancing between their hives amongst the trees at the bottom of the garden.

Birds whistled and swooped from branch to branch, and a river glinted in the sunlight. A small white dog curled up between the sisters' feet, fast asleep, and Mad Dog felt like sleeping too. He closed his eyes, and might well have dropped off if Uncle hadn't turned up.

He was politer than Mr Griffiths, but no less angry. 'You've got some explaining to do,' he said. 'Do you realise what you've put us through? We all thought that you were dead. Aunty's been beside herself, and so have I and so has your school. Do you know, there are parents threatening to take their children away because they think the teaching staff aren't competent? And other parents threatening to sue. And all because of you. *What've you got to say for yourself?*'

Mad Dog hung his head. 'If I got lost, it was my own fault, not the school's or anybody else's,' he said.

'So that's what you call it?' Uncle said. '*Getting lost*.'

'I don't know what else to call it,' Mad Dog said.

'Try *mucking about*. Try *not listening to your teacher*. Try *wandering off and doing the opposite of what you're told*,' Uncle said.

He collected Mad Dog's belongings from the house, thanked the sisters for all they'd done and frog-marched him out to the car. But at the last minute, instead of getting into it, Mad Dog hung back. He wanted to go home – of course he did, no matter how much trouble he was in. But he didn't want to leave this peaceful garden where he had felt safe.

But he had no choice. Uncle packed him into the car and the sisters came and stood round it, wishing him all the best. One of them gave Uncle directions for a short cut back over the mountain, avoiding the main pass road, and the other seized the opportunity of Uncle's being distracted to lean through the open window and tell Mad Dog that Plynlimon might be full of tricks, but it was a wonderful mountain too.

'Some people go up there and never feel a thing,' she said in a low voice, as if for his ears alone. 'But some go up there and Plynlimon comes alive for them. And that's what happened to you, isn't it? Well, there's a treasure on that mountain, if you're brave enough to look for it. You mark my words. *It's up there, waiting to be found*.'

20

Answers for Elvis

When Mad Dog got home, Uncle wasn't the only one who was furious. Everyone was furious, right down to Aunty's kitchen ladies, Ruth and Kathleen, who'd been up with her all night long, making drinks and manning the phones.

Even Elvis was furious, leaping out and punching Mad Dog in the stomach the moment he climbed out of Uncle's car, as if to punish him for all he'd put him through. Then, no sooner had they got into the house, than Mrs Heligan phoned up, seeming to think Mad Dog had done the whole thing deliberately to get at her.

Even the police had to be faced, who wanted to get Mad Dog's story straight and tell him how much the search for him had cost.

Then finally Aunty – who was rarely a woman lost for words – told Mad Dog what she thought of him. '*Do you realise what you've done?*' she said for the whole world to hear, including her guests. 'How much pain and grief you've caused? How much trouble you've put people to? Really Ryan, what were you *thinking* of? HOW DARE YOU PULL A STUNT LIKE THAT?'

Mad Dog baulked at that word *stunt*. He knew he'd behaved thoughtlessly, but that was all it had been, and it would have been nice if Aunty could have been pleased to have him back. Getting lost wasn't something he'd done on purpose to cause a fuss. He tried explaining this, but Aunty said that, if it hadn't been on purpose, how else would he describe it?

'I suppose your legs just took off on their own!' she said. 'And Grendel's legs along with you. Because this isn't only about you, is it? She got lost as well, and not only have we had our own fears to contend with but we've had Grendel's father breathing fire all over us, threatening what he'd do if you as much as harmed a hair of his princess's head!'

For days after that, Mad Dog kept trying to find ways to say sorry, but nobody seemed interested. Elvis's fear of losing him had turned into a total refusal to have anything to do with him. Aunty said she'd got no time for apologies because she had a business to run. Uncle said that words were cheap.

Mad Dog even tried apologising to Ruth and Kathleen, in the hope that they at least could find it in their hearts to show a bit of sympathy. But they were no more impressed than anybody else. 'You think you're in trouble now,' they said. 'But you wait until your school gets hold of you. There'll be hell to pay when you get back!'

They were right. Mad Dog only had to walk across the playground to find himself a major spectacle. Grendel and her gang glared at him as if he were evil incarnate. Mad Dog shuddered at the memory of their night together and wondered what she'd told her friends. Certainly, Luke, Hippie and Rhys teased him mercilessly about his 'sweetheart' and blew kisses at him every time Grendel was around.

Everybody had it in for him. Teachers stared coldly at him. The head teacher had him in his office and tore him off a strip with Aunty and Uncle present. Even a representative of the search-and-rescue services came into school to tell a special assembly what they thought of little boys who went wandering off by themselves on lonely mountains. Afterwards the representative had words in private with Mad Dog, and then words with Mrs Heligan too, who came out looking furious. The talk around the school was that her job was on the line.

Nobody, however, was as furious as Mrs Anwen Jones. Lovely Mrs Anwen Jones – Mad Dog's favourite teacher ever, who might have had food poisoning on the day in question, but had put hours of careful thought into that trip, and was distraught about the way things had turned out. Around school, people said there'd been a massive bust-up between her and Mrs Heligan, and that they weren't talking any more.

But she certainly had plenty to say to Mad Dog. 'That trip was meant to be a *treat*,' she said in a controlled but very scary voice, when she got him on his own. 'But you had to go and mess it up, didn't you? One small boy doing his own thing, and the whole thing's ruined for everybody else! Well, Ryan Lewis, I want you to know that if you as much as blink without permission from now until the end of term, you're *for it*.'

As if to give Mad Dog a foretaste of what being *for it* meant, Mrs Anwen Jones slapped him in detention for the next week and said he was lucky not to be suspended. Here he was forced to write an account of what had happened on the mountain, where he'd gone wrong and why he'd never do it again. Then he had to copy it out, and then copy it again. *Drafting* was what Mrs Anwen Jones called it – an important exercise in the National Curriculum, and he should thank her for giving him the chance to improve his skills. But Mad Dog had a string of other words for it, none of which were in the National Curriculum, and none of which were repeatable.

On the last day of what was not only his last term but his whole life in that school, Mad Dog handed in his efforts. By lunchtime, Mrs Anwen Jones had it back to him with '*sloppy work – untidy handwriting – bad spelling – you'll have to pull your socks up when you start at the comprehensive*' written all over it.

It was a far cry from the ticks on Mad Dog's Rheidol project, and hardly the way he'd imagined saying goodbye to his favourite teacher. For the rest of the day, he skulked around pretending he couldn't see the way that people were looking at him. Ever since coming back off the mountain, he'd been a marked man, and this last day was no different.

The day ended with a leavers' service which everybody attended. Afterwards it was a relief to get away. The rest of the class was crying, hugging each other, giving presents and taking photographs. But Mad Dog got into Aunty's car without looking at anybody, and didn't even relent when Mrs Anwen Jones came over and said, 'All the best then, Ryan.'

'Thanks,' he muttered, staring straight ahead of him. Aunty drove away and he didn't look back, not even once.

For days after that, Mad Dog skulked around the vardo, which wasn't the most exciting place to spend a summer holiday but was better than school. Most of his time was spent on an old PlayStation that Uncle had brought home from work in the harbour office. Mad Dog had never shown the slightest interest in computer games before, but now he took to the PlayStation like a holed boat to a dry dock. With a screen in front of him and a controller in his hand, he didn't have to think about anything, least of all what had *really* happened up there on Plynlimon.

At night-time however, in the dark, with nothing to distract Mad Dog, the whole thing would come creeping back. Had something *really* chased him up there on the mountain? And, if not, why the panic? And why had that ruined cottage scared him so much? And that crossroads between valleys – why, when he'd turned back, had it looked so shockingly familiar?

Even the good bits about Plynlimon left Mad Dog with questions. Turquoise gadflies, bright pink foxgloves and strings of ponds were all very well but why had he found himself so captivated by them? Why so easily had they cast their spell? And his *ffon* – the way he'd lost it and it had turned up again? What had that all been about? And that thing Grendel said about the light – what had *that* been about?

Mad Dog had no answers, and he wished the questions would go away. One thing was for certain, though – the world beyond his computer screen was a dangerous place, and it was best to stay indoors where it was safe.

Hardly surprisingly, it turned out to be a long summer holiday. Jobs around the hotel shaped a fair part of it, and the PlayStation and television shaped the rest. Mad Dog's friends phoned, apologising for making fun of him and trying to persuade him to come down and play. Aunty's sisters phoned as well. Even though they hardly talked to Aunty any more, they still wanted Mad Dog to come and play, and said their sons were missing him. But Aunty said he wouldn't come, and she wasn't being awkward. It was true.

At some point during the holidays, Mad Dog wrote to the Ingram sisters thanking them for what they'd done for him and sending back their clothes. He never thought he'd hear from them again, and didn't particularly want to either, but a letter came straight back. It didn't say much, but it smelt of flowers and brought back memories of being rescued and feeling safe. He remembered sitting in the sisters' garden, lapping up the sunshine and drinking amber tea, and he remembered what they'd said about treasure on Plynlimon and people finding it if they were brave enough.

There was nothing brave about hiding in a caravan, but Mad Dog threw away the sisters' letter, telling himself that he didn't want to think about things like treasure, and being brave and mountains coming alive. If he never saw Plynlimon again it would be too soon for him, and the same went for the River Rheidol. He mightn't know for sure what river had flowed through that crossroad between the valleys, but he only had to think about it to not want to see the Rheidol ever again. It didn't feel like a friend any more. It didn't feel safe. Once there'd been comfort in the idea of one river running through Mad Dog's life. But Mad Dog had lost his faith in rivers. If he never saw one again, it would have been too soon.

So Mad Dog kept out of the way of the Rheidol. An entire summer holiday went by without him going down to it even once. But the questions persisted, no matter what he did. His time on Plynlimon Mountain had unlocked something in him from which he couldn't escape.

Sometimes Mad Dog felt as if he was standing on the edge of a precipice with every unanswered question and forgotten memory in his entire life on the other side. 'Why can't I just live an ordinary life?' he asked himself one day. 'You know, wake up, get up, go out to play, come in again, have a good time, never think too much, never question things, simply just – oh, I don't know, just *be*? Why's my life got to be such a mystery?'

Mad Dog stared down at his *ffon*. Its intricately engraved topknot stared back at him with its moons, stars and bundle of letters spelling out a message that he'd never understood. WAOOC. Yet another mystery that he'd failed to unlock! Mad Dog's eyes ran over the letters, trying to work them out. Maybe they were unreadable because they had no meaning. Maybe they were just a bunch of shapes, and didn't spell out anything and there was nothing to unlock.

Mad Dog fetched a piece of paper and tried again, mixing up the letters to see if something new emerged. He expected nothing, but it was worth a try. If he could only crack this one small code, he told himself, then maybe he could crack some of the bigger mysteries in his life. Maybe one would lead him to the next, in a chain effect.

But WOOAC meant no more to him than AWOOC, WAOCO, CAOOW, CWOOA, OWAOC or any other combination that Mad Dog came up with. And giving the letters numbers made no difference either. Even treating the word as a picture and standing it every way round, including on its head, made no difference.

'What are you doing?' Elvis said.

He'd come in from playing at a friend's house down in the village. Mad Dog hardly ever saw him any more, and it wasn't just because Elvis was still upset with him for getting lost. Devil's Bridge was his home now. He had his own friends and they had their dens. He never played with Mad Dog, or hung around with him or talked about their life at No. 3. And he definitely never talked about their old life before No. 3.

'I'm trying to work out what this means,' Mad Dog said, thrusting his *ffon* at Elvis.

Elvis pushed it back. 'Why would I be interested in that old thing?' he said.

Mad Dog felt his hackles rising. 'It's not an *old thing*,' he said. 'It's a message from our parents.'

Elvis shrugged. 'So what?' he said.

Mad Dog was shocked. 'You shouldn't talk like that. Not about our parents. Our parents *loved* us, and you ought to give them some respect.'

Elvis looked unimpressed. 'Where are they now?' he said. 'I can't respect someone I've never met.'

'They had to go away,' Mad Dog said.

'Why did they do that?'

'I don't know.'

Elvis shrugged again, as if to say *there you are*, and stomped off, leaving Mad Dog frustrated at his lack of interest. But one day things would change, he knew. His brother would grow up, and then he'd want to know everything. Who their parents were. What had happened to them. Where they'd come from. Why they had abandoned them.

He wouldn't always walk away. And if Mad Dog –
who'd been there at the time, and lived through it all
– didn't have the answers, then his brother would
want to know why.

Part IV
The Vasty Deep

21

Returning to Plynlimon

Halfway through August, the weather turned nasty. A series of squally storms hit Devil's Bridge and there was thunder at night and rain every day. Hotel guests turned tetchy, and Aunty said that as far as she was concerned her honeymoon period in the hotel business was definitely over. Complaints were made about stupid things that hadn't bothered guests before, and it wasn't helped by the kitchen ladies making a series of silly blunders, like serving new potatoes uncooked to table and putting desserts that were meant for the cooler in the warming oven instead.

Even out in the vardo, Mad Dog caught the general mood of tetchiness. He'd sit at the window, staring at the back of the hotel and watching rain coming down in sheets, telling himself that he hated Devil's Bridge and wishing that he was back at No. 3. When Aunty came in, he'd snap at her. When Uncle tried to talk to him, he wouldn't answer. When Elvis looked his way, he'd say, 'What are you staring at? Haven't you got something better to do with your time?'

The feeling around the family was that Mad Dog was turning adolescent and couldn't help himself. But if his age was getting to him, it certainly wasn't the only thing. For starters there was a new school to worry about, beginning in a few weeks' time. And then there were all those questions about his past lodged inside Mad Dog's head.

Even when the rain clouds blew away, his mood stayed sour and grumpy. All over Devil's Bridge, wet roads steamed in the sunshine, trees drip-dried and Aunty's guests cheered up and started venturing outside. Suddenly the landscape they'd thought so grey and lacklustre shone like a jewel that they wanted to wear.

'Thank God for that!' said Aunty, who'd had enough of guests under her feet all day long. 'They've gone at last!'

She suggested that Mad Dog might like to do the same, instead of moping around the vardo all day and sitting up late watching rubbish on the telly. Why didn't he play with the children in the village? It would do him good, she said, and some of them would be going to the same comprehensive in the autumn, so it would be a chance to make friends.

But Mad Dog moped around indoors, ignoring all Aunty's advice. The only place where he felt truly safe was inside the vardo where the outside world couldn't get at him. Late-night horror movies on the telly were as nothing compared to leaves drying on trees or the smell of grass warming up. Mad Dog didn't want to see open hilltops any more, or forests, or the river glinting like gold down in the bottom of the gorge. These things were part of a world that scared him too much.

Even that evening, when the guests came out into the garden to eat beneath the rising moon, Mad Dog didn't want to go outside. Instead he shut his window, drew his curtains, built himself a brand new barricade, as if danger was imminent, and climbed into his bed. Not that he could get to sleep. The night was muggy, and the vardo was stuffy at the best of times. Even later, after Aunty and Uncle had come to bed, the vardo was still as hot as a tin can.

In the end, Mad Dog got up to fetch a glass of water and open a couple of windows. He opened the front door as well, and the moon was shining over the hotel. It was as round and perfect as a cup of milk, and its silvery light flooded across the garden.

After weeks indoors, its impact was instant and overwhelming. Mad Dog stood watching patterns of light and shade stretching down the lawn, across the road and into the wood. And it was in those moments that he was lost.

Suddenly, scarcely knowing what he was doing, Mad Dog found himself flinging on clothes, struggling into trainers and heading out into the moonlight. He never meant to go any further than the edge of the garden – but that wasn't how things ended up.

When Mad Dog reached the edge of the garden, the road beyond it looked like a silver river calling him away. The wood looked silver too, its paths mosaics of light and shade. Mad Dog started down them without a second thought. When he reached the bottom of the valley and saw the river in front of him, he tore off his trainers, strung them round his neck and waded straight in.

No danger was down here in the wood. There was nothing to scare him. Why he'd stayed indoors all summer long, he didn't know. Feeling ridiculous for every minute he'd wasted in the vardo, Mad Dog started heading upstream.

The whole thing happened as smoothly as stepping on to an escalator. It was good to be back. Good beyond words. Mad Dog picked his way through pools, discovering them again like old friends. It was far too magical a night for sweating in his tin-can bed. Instead he climbed over boulders and let the river lead him up to Parson's Bridge, where he'd broken his leg, then on beyond it.

Never for a moment did he think he'd gone too far, or contemplate turning back. He was captivated by the moonlight, and the river seemed to call him on. Even in the darkest places he followed it, as if a thread of light could be traced through its deep waters.

By dawn, Mad Dog had passed through the village of Ponterwyd, up on the main Aberystwyth road, and come out the other side. Here the deep gorges of the Vale of Rheidol fell behind him and the landscape opened out, revealing the landmass of Plynlimon. All summer long Mad Dog had hidden from it, and now here it was again.

For the first time since setting out, Mad Dog found himself shivering. There was no doubt where he'd been heading throughout the night, and he wished he'd thought to bring his *ffon*. The moon no longer wove its strange enchantment over him but even so, here in the clear light of morning, he knew he had to carry on. No longer was this just some midnight madness. It was the journey he'd been on all summer. Even shut up in the vardo, he'd been on this journey. And before this summer – before Plynlimon, and the school trip – he'd been on it even then.

Mad Dog strode towards Plynlimon, telling himself to be brave and do what his mother had always called 'trust in the power of the open road'. Not that he'd ever known what that had meant. It had just been one of those weird little phrases that had stuck inside his head.

Now, however, it made sense. All the answers to his questions were somewhere on the road ahead. He was sure they were, at a crossroads between valleys, beside a ruined cottage.

Mad Dog shivered again. 'Every time I ever ran away,' he said out loud, 'it was for this. It wasn't just for mermaids that I went off, or to find my parents or because I took the wrong track on a school trip. I went off to solve a mystery. And maybe my parents are caught up in it, and maybe they aren't. Maybe there's a treasure at the end of it, like the Ingram sisters said. But it's the mystery that I've been hiding from all my life and I've got to face it, *because it won't go away*.'

The sun broke over the hills. Trees and hedges filled up with gold and birds sang all around Mad Dog. Back in the vardo, the only thing singing would be Aunty's alarm, awakening her to find him gone. But, here on the road back to Plynlimon, he didn't give her a moment's thought. He was too busy striding up the road, following the Rheidol back to his past and the answers to his questions.

Even when exhaustion overwhelmed him, Mad Dog wouldn't stop. He reached the dam that held back Nant y Moch, and started down towards the lake, telling himself it was only a short distance. But distances can be deceptive on country roads, especially the roads around Plynlimon with their endless dips and dells.

It was hours later that Mad Dog finally reached the place where the school bus had pulled up. Plynlimon spread out before him, but he could go no further. By now he'd been travelling all night and half the morning, and he felt exhausted.

Mad Dog picked a path down to the top end of the lake, where the Rheidol flowed into it. Here, in a peaty overhang that appeared, from its wealth of fleece, to be a popular resting place for local sheep, he curled up, made himself comfortable and drifted off to sleep.

Later he awoke to find that the sun had moved across the sky, casting the river before him in a whole new light. By now the day was hot – a classic summer's day, perfect for everything but being out in the sun. Mad Dog started up the valley with not a tree in sight to give him any shelter. The road lay far behind him now, and he had only his instincts to guide him. That and the river, of course. He tried to stick to it, but the grasslands that he was striding through were so bunched and thick that he could scarcely see where the river ran any more.

Mad Dog wasn't used to sunshine after weeks inside the vardo. He was hungry too, and his legs were aching with the effort of struggling through long grass without falling over. A whole network of waterways ran beneath his feet. He could hear them, but they were almost impossible to see, and it was getting increasingly difficult to work out which – if any of them – led in the direction of the Rheidol.

Things were slowly going wrong, and Mad Dog couldn't put them right. Hills folded in around him, valley following valley, but none leading to the crossroads between them that he was looking for. For a while Plynlimon Fawr would be on one side of him and he'd think, from the Google map inside his head, that he knew where he was. But then he'd suddenly discover that Plynlimon Fawr was on the other side of him, and he wouldn't have a clue how it had got there.

The valleys were enormous too, great glacial sweeps of grassland with high hills standing over them. Lost amongst them, Mad Dog felt small and insignificant – one dot of a boy in a vast wilderness that rolled on for ever.

Finally the sun started lowering in the sky. It was a relief not to be so hot any more, but Mad Dog realised he was facing yet another night out in the open. The air was soft and warm, but darkness lay not far ahead and Mad Dog wasn't dressed for a night out in the open.

A cold moon rose over the hills, and it didn't look silvery this time. It looked bone-white and utterly without enchantment. Mad Dog searched around for somewhere dry to lay himself down, and found it in the form of an enormous boulder with a flattish top, which he knew from his Rheidol project was called a *roche moutonnée*.

It hardly looked what he'd call comfortable but, with no other way of keeping dry for the night, Mad Dog climbed on to the boulder and prayed for the ease with which he'd fallen asleep earlier.

Hardly surprisingly, it wasn't exactly the best of nights. Mad Dog's legs ached from all that walking and his skin burned from the sun. His belly gnawed with hunger and he slept sporadically, haunted by dreams of death and battle, blood and fire. If the Red Judge of Plynlimon had been after him, he couldn't have had a more restless night.

22

Dancers in the Dawn

Next morning, Mad Dog awoke to birdsong. He opened his eyes to find the valley filling with light, as if just for him. And why not, he thought. He deserved it. Getting through not just one night on Plynlimon, but now another one as well, made him a hero.

It was a morning for heroes too. Mad Dog sat on his boulder, watching the sky turning blue and the stars fading one by one. He could see for miles all around him. A little strand of mist had attached itself to the valley floor but, above it, everything was crystal clear.

Mad Dog looked up the valley and a thin band of light which looked like daybreak in the wrong place caught his attention. At first he thought it must be sunlight striking water, but then it started growing. It started coming down the valley towards him, melting the mist and shimmering as it approached.

What was going on? Mad Dog's first thought was that the valley was flooding, but then he thought it might have caught on fire. Either way he slid behind the boulder as if for protection. Slowly the band of light drew closer and he heard music caught up in it, and saw people in the golden light – a whole procession of them, playing instruments, dancing, ringing hand-bells and carrying what Mad Dog could now see were flaming torches.

Mad Dog came out from behind his boulder to

watch. There was nothing here to be afraid of. No fire to burn the valley after all, no flood to drown it and not even anything to fear from the dancers. They weren't like those other ones he'd seen years before, swirling around the Aged Relative's conservatory, lit by tall black candles. Those dancers had been like a chain-gang, trapped behind their masks. But these people danced like free spirits.

As they drew closer, Mad Dog saw open faces, not a mask in sight, and red-and-white striped coats, as bright as flames, gathered at elbows and hanging loosely off people's backs. He saw red-and-white stockings with red and white roses on red and white shoes. He saw red-and-white ribbons on wrists and in hair, and red-and-white caps that had been decorated with beads and feathers.

Who were these people, Mad Dog asked himself, and what were they doing here in this lonely place? He didn't know but, when the procession drew level with him, it stopped and everybody turned his way. Mad Dog stood before it, not knowing what to expect. There were children in the procession, and old people and every age of person in between, and they all smiled and waved at him and raised their caps.

Mad Dog waved back, noticing for the first time that a column of soldiers stood at the back of the procession, carrying weapons and bearing battered standards. Some wore white feathers in their helmets and some wore red. But all of them stood proud and tall and, when everybody else waved and raised their caps, they raised their helmets and waved too, and Mad Dog couldn't have felt more honoured if he'd been at the New Millennium Stadium in Cardiff, playing rugby for Wales before a crowd of thousands.

He took a step towards the procession, and all the singing, dancing and bell-ringing ceased, the instruments stopped playing, the waving stopped and the flaming torches were lowered. Then two of the soldiers, looking little more than children, stepped forward. Both were pale. Both were wounded, Mad Dog noticed. Each took a feather out of his helmet – one white, one red – and held them out to Mad Dog as if offering him a choice. The entire procession watched to see what he would do.

Mad Dog looked at the feathers and didn't have a clue. Looked at the soldiers and didn't have a clue. Looked around at everybody else, and *still* didn't have a clue, but understood that in some way, beyond what he could fathom, this moment was significant.

The soldiers thrust their feathers at him again, as if time was passing and a decision needed to be made. But what decision? What was the choice? Red could be for lifeblood and white for death. Or red for courage and white for cowardice. Or red could even be for Wales and white for England, and this corner of Plynlimon could be the selfsame Glyn Hyddgen where the great Owain Glyndwr had defeated the English and, according to Shakespeare, called forth 'spirits from the vasty deep'.

Mad Dog shivered. He looked at the procession and wondered if they were such spirits – the elves and fairy folk he'd read about when he'd done his research on Plynlimon – or if they were the dead in battle, left behind to haunt this place. But, whoever they might be, there was still a choice to be made, and it wasn't theirs – it was his.

What if I take both? Mad Dog reckoned, looking from one feather to the other. Who's to say I shouldn't? Or if I refuse to make a choice and simply walk away? What difference would it make?

In the end, however, Mad Dog chose the white feather. It would have been nice to say he'd done it for a reason but, ever afterwards, he'd always know it could just as easily have gone the other way.

But the choice seemed to please everybody, whatever it meant. The flaming torches were raised again and the entire procession – red and white alike, dancers, singers, musicians and soldiers – clapped, cheered, hooted, hollered and threw their caps, helmets and even the odd standard up in the air.

Mad Dog didn't have a clue what they were so pleased about. He pocketed the feather and the procession reformed. The singing started up again, along with the ringing of bells and playing of instruments. Then the procession took its leave, disappearing down the valley, and, if Plynlimon ever came alive, like the Ingram sisters had said, it couldn't have got more alive than this.

23

White Porcelain Cups

For hours after that, Mad Dog was on a high. He didn't understand what had just happened, but he didn't feel stiff any more, or cold or hungry. For hours he wandered over Plynlimon, never thinking where he was going, or looking for crossroads between valleys or answers to questions. The mystery of his past meant nothing compared to what had just happened to him. He climbed, jumped, ran, swam, scuffed up stones, skipped over peat bogs and sang with the larks. No longer was he Ryan Lewis, but he was Mad Dog Moonlight again, come back to life as if set free.

Only later in the day did Mad Dog start thinking like his old Ryan self. He was standing on a high point overlooking the main pass road. The sun was shining on a string of cars and lorries snaking their way down to Aberystwyth and suddenly, like coming in to land from a long sea voyage, he wanted home again. Mountaintop experiences were all very well, but what he wanted was ordinary life – and, by ordinary life, he didn't mean the Falls Hotel, he meant No. 3.

Suddenly Mad Dog's thoughts turned to the Gap and the barge den, his friends and football on the grass, the Rheidol running through the harbour and Aunty's kitchen full of food. *Food.* He hadn't felt hungry before but now, he realised, he was starving.

Mad Dog watched a bus come down the pass road, glinting in the afternoon sun, and wished himself on board, heading home to No. 3. He knew that Aunty wouldn't be there, but it made no difference. He started heading down the mountain, anyway.

An hour later, when he reached the road, the bus had long since gone, of course. He stood on the verge, waiting for another one to come along. Cars and lorries went past, but no further buses appeared, and no one took any notice of him until a woman came over from a little country inn just up the road.

'You do know, don't you, that the last bus has gone for today?' she said. 'Are you heading for Aberystwyth?'

Mad Dog said he was.

'I'm going there myself,' she said. 'I could give you a lift – if you wanted, that is. Or you could come into the inn and phone for someone to collect you.'

Mad Dog accepted the lift. The woman asked where he wanted to be dropped off, and he told her down by the harbour. Aunty would kill him, he knew, for going with a stranger. But then she was going to kill him anyway, when she finally got her hands on him, so what difference did it make?

'You all right?' the woman said, as he sat in total silence down the hairpin bends of the pass road. 'I'm not making you feel car sick, or anything like that?'

'I'm fine,' Mad Dog said.

But he didn't feel fine. His legs throbbed, his head ached and he felt giddy with hunger.

The woman dropped Mad Dog at the end of the Gap. He barely thanked her before heading off. There was only one thing on his mind, and that was Aunty's fridge. Before he got very far, however, a sign caught his attention, fixed right in the middle of No. 3's garden. And when Mad Dog saw it, he forgot hunger and just about everything else.

FOR SALE.

How could that be?

Mad Dog raced down the Gap, flung open the gate, hauled the sign out of the ground and broke it in half. Then, in his efforts to get inside and tear a second sign out of his bedroom window, he almost battered in the front door. This couldn't be happening, he thought, shutting it behind him and drinking in the smell of home. Aunty and Uncle had promised! They'd be back in the autumn. That's what they'd said. This was business, they'd said, but No. 3 was their home. It always would be. On their word of honour they'd promised him.

Crying tears of helpless fury, Mad Dog tore upstairs and dragged the second FOR SALE sign out of his bedroom window. But even without it there any more, nothing in the house felt right.

'How could they do this to me?' Mad Dog cried. 'How could they do this to No. 3?'

He'd never again trust Aunty and Uncle. And he'd certainly never go back to them! He'd go back up Plynlimon, he told himself, and live like a wild boy, eating berries and making snares the way his dad used to do in the old days, and catching fish with his hands.

Mad Dog crouched at his bedroom window, hidden behind the curtains so that nobody would see him. It was a perfect summer's evening – at least for everybody else. He could hear voices calling to each other across the marina and see boats coming in and out. He dropped off to sleep, exhausted and overwhelmed with emotion.

When he awoke, the harbour had fallen silent and

nothing was moving any more apart from one final boat that was making its way down past the pontoons like a shadow in advance of night. He watched it cut across the Rheidol and head for the Gap. Usually it was only local folk who moored in the Gap, but Mad Dog didn't recognise this boat and the people who came off it were total strangers.

He watched them come ashore, expecting them to hurry off into town like all the other yacht marina people did. But they sauntered along the Gap as if they had all the time in the world. Their arms were around each other and they were laughing. When they reached the gate to No. 3, they stopped and looked at the FOR SALE sign lying broken on the ground. Mad Dog waited for them to carry on but, after glancing at each other and saying something he couldn't hear, they opened the gate and started up the path.

At the sight of potential buyers, come to snoop around the house, Mad Dog didn't think twice. Nobody – *nobody* – was going to buy No. 3! Like the master of a ship preparing to repel boarders, he tore downstairs and crouched behind the front door as if the hall was under attack. A bell rang, its sound shrilling through the house. Then the letterbox fluttered and Mad Dog caught sight of a pair of eyes peering through it.

Mercifully they didn't see him crouched behind the door. 'It looks like no one lives here any more,' he heard a woman's voice say. Then he caught a glimpse of the two of them starting round the side of the house as if looking for a back way in. Immediately he raced down the hall to the kitchen – but arrived too late.

'*What d'you think you're doing?*' Mad Dog yelled,

as the strangers came strolling in as if they owned the place. 'This is private property! You're trespassing. *Get out!*'

The strangers looked surprised, to put it mildly. Mad Dog shouted that if it was a house they were after they could go and buy another one somewhere else. They said they didn't want to buy the house, and were sorry for trespassing, but all they were doing was looking for old friends.

'Well, you've come to the wrong place!' Mad Dog said, marching to the kitchen door and holding it open.

The strangers headed for the door as if they couldn't get out fast enough. But then right at the last minute, one of them – an elfin-faced young woman with sharp, sparkling eyes – said, 'Hang on. We *haven't* made a mistake. The decoration's different, but remember drying our things on that stove? And our trunk opened out there in the middle of the floor? And look on that shelf. Look up there. *Those are our cups.*'

Mad Dog looked where the woman was pointing. On Aunty's top shelf, where she kept the things she never used, sat a stack of white porcelain cups that had been there so long that he'd all but forgotten them.

'What do you mean, *your* cups?' he said.

The woman crossed the floor and got one down. Inside it, beneath a thick coat of dust, she found a fifty-pound note, which she handed to her companion.

'Remember this?' she said.

He said he did. 'It was this house,' he said.

'What house?' Mad Dog said.

'And you must be Ryan,' the man said. 'Little Ryan Lewis, all grown up. Don't you remember us?'

He smiled at Mad Dog, but Mad Dog glared back. He didn't know any Ryans, he said, and most definitely didn't remember these strangers. They weren't like anyone he'd ever known, and any even remotely passing resemblance to sailors he remembered from years ago was a coincidence. Those sailors had been old, and battered by the sea, but these ones were far too young for the sorts of stories that Mad Dog remembered them telling him, keeping him on the edge of his seat. They weren't hardened mariners like those other sailors had been. And they didn't have the ocean in their eyes.

But then the woman stepped forward and held out her hand, and it was a sailor's hand, seasoned by all weathers, and her eyes – when she fixed them on Mad Dog – were full of secret things that set his pulse racing.

'My name's Abren,' she said. 'I can't remember if I ever told you that. And he's Phaze II, which is a funny sort of name, I grant you, but there's a story behind it, and maybe you'll get him to tell it one day. I don't see why not – you've heard half his other tales, as I'm sure you will remember.'

She looked at Mad Dog as if willing him to remember. And, yes, there *was* something about her that he recognised, and it came to him that, if she'd seemed older once, it would have been because he'd seen her through the eyes of a much younger child.

'You're not ... I mean ... you're not *the sailors*?' he said.

She laughed at that. They both did. 'Well, I always

dreamt of being a *seafarer*,' the man said. 'It had a ring to it, I seemed to think. But *sailor* will do, at least for now. It's as good a word as any, and better than some.'

24

Broken

That night, Mad Dog ate supper in the sailors' cabin on their boat. They sat on one berth and he sat opposite them, scoffing as if there was no tomorrow. All around them, the harbour was still and quiet, not another soul in sight. Mad Dog felt as if the three of them were bound together by some strange twist of fate that had brought them together, against all odds, just when he needed it.

All he could think about – apart from food – was the sailors taking him away with them. He'd dreamt about it when he was a little boy, imagining life on the open seas. And now that Aunty and Uncle had betrayed him, it was the only thing he wanted.

Before the subject could be broached, however, there were questions that had to be answered. What had he been doing, the sailors wanted to know, since they'd last met? And Aunty, Uncle and baby Eric – how were they? And why was No. 3 empty? Why was it for sale? And what had Mad Dog been doing there, all alone? *And why was he so hungry?*

Mad Dog laughed when they asked that – and took another helping. He told them all about Aunty inheriting the Falls Hotel from the Aged Relative, and about her betraying him by selling No. 3. But he didn't tell them about Plynlimon or the strange procession he had seen, or the feather in his pocket or anything like that.

Finally the subject came round to parents. The sailors said they hadn't realised that Aunty and Uncle were any other than Mad Dog's real mum and dad.

'We never picked up that you were adopted,' they said.

'I'm not adopted,' Mad Dog said.

'So what's your story, then?' the sailors said.

What *was* his story? Mad Dog shrugged. It was the most natural question in the world, but he didn't have the answer.

'All I know,' he said, 'is that one day I had parents just like everybody else, and my name was Mad Dog Moonlight. And the next I didn't, and my name was Ryan Lewis and I lived with Aunty and Uncle in a house I'd never seen before. I don't remember anything before I got there, only what I was told, which is that the police had found me. I remember them bringing me to No. 3, but I can't remember where I came from, or anything like that. And mostly I feel fine about it, but sometimes – especially recently – I don't.'

Mad Dog paused and looked up. The sailors were sitting absolutely still. There was a concentration about them that was total, as if they were hanging on to his every word. When he'd finished, Abren said that she too had lost her memory once but that, in the end, it had come back.

'There's something very mysterious about the things we choose to forget,' she said. 'And the process of remembering is even stranger. But these things happen when they're ready. You can't rush them. You have to wait.'

Mad Dog said he'd waited long enough, and asked

what had brought back Abren's memory. She said that, strangely enough, it had been a mountain.

Mad Dog felt himself go cold all over. 'What mountain?' he said – but it didn't take much to guess.

'*Plynlimon Mountain*,' Abren said. 'Why are you looking at me like that? What's the matter? Do you know it?'

Mad Dog didn't answer, not at first. Then, haltingly, he tried his best. Not only did he know Plynlimon, he said, but he also knew that it was tied up with his past.

'I can't explain how,' he said. 'And I can't explain why. But there's a secret on that mountain waiting to be found, and I'm a part of it. I know I am.'

If the night had seemed quiet before, it was deathly silent now. The sailors leant towards Mad Dog, listening intently, their faces grave but giving little away. He told them about the dancers, but didn't show them the feather. He told them about getting lost on the school trip, and Plynlimon casting its spell on him, and he even told them about the ruined cottage, and the hillock and the crossroads between valleys. The only time that either of them interrupted him was when he told them what the Ingram sisters had said about people going up Plynlimon and never coming back.

'Some people come back, but they never really get away,' Abren said – but she didn't explain what she meant by that.

Mad Dog shivered.

'You're frightened of Plynlimon, aren't you?' Phaze II said.

Was he frightened of the mountain? Or was it

something on it that frightened him? Mad Dog wasn't sure, but he told the sailors about his long flight with Grendel in tow, imagining being chased.

'I wouldn't be so sure that you were imagining it,' Phaze II said.

'What do you mean?' Mad Dog said.

'You're not the only one who's been chased across Plynlimon,' Phaze II said. 'I have too, and so has Abren.'

Mad Dog stared at them, wondering what strange fate had brought the three of them together. The sailors looked back as if they were wondering the same thing. Then, as if this conversation had gone quite far enough, thank you very much, Abren got to her feet. Storms couldn't shake her – wild seas, broken boats, nights of peril on the ocean couldn't shake her. But this talk of Plynlimon could.

She started clearing away dishes, and put a kettle on the stove. Phaze II made a pot of hot black coffee and suggested that they might like to drink it under the stars. Mad Dog followed them up on to the deck where the night looked perfect for running away to sea. Silvery and bright. A mermaid night. An anything-could-happen-and-I'm-up-for-it night. A new beginnings night, where Mad Dog could put Plynlimon behind him, just like the sailors appeared to have done, and never talk about it again.

He braced himself to ask the sailors if he could go with them. 'All these years, I never forgot you, you know,' he began, wanting them to agree that their meeting again was no coincidence.

'We've never forgotten you either,' the sailors replied. But they didn't say anything about being bound together or having a future, and they definitely didn't say anything about him going with them. Instead they started on about wonderful Aunty and Uncle were and how lucky Mad Dog was to have them for foster parents.

This conversation definitely wasn't going the way that Mad Dog wanted. Abren said that Uncle and Aunty must be worrying about where he was, but Mad Dog insisted that they didn't deserve to know.

'Whatever they've done,' said Abren, 'and however you feel about them, they need to know you're safe. You could always use our phone. Or we could even hire a taxi and take you back. It would be for the best. Don't you think?'

Mad Dog thought that no way, ever, was he going back. 'You don't understand,' he said. 'You haven't heard what I've been saying. I've got to be free. Free for adventures, just like you. I've always known that you'd come back. *I want to go with you.*'

The sailors smiled as if it was a nice idea, but simply not possible. Abren agreed that it was a strange coincidence that had brought them back, just when Mad Dog needed them. But they would always be friends, she said. It wasn't something that depended on his going with them.

While she was speaking, Phaze II got on the phone to the Falls Hotel. Aunty's relief could be heard right across the harbour. For a moment, she couldn't think straight and wanted to come and get Mad Dog. Then she said that perhaps it would be better if he spent the night at one of her sisters' houses, as it was so late. Then she said she wanted him back anyway, late or not, and never mind her sisters – the sailors should put him in a taxi and she'd pay for it when he arrived.

After that, everything happened very quickly. A taxi was called for and suddenly it was time to go.

'You don't understand,' Mad Dog protested as the sailors tried to coax him into it. 'I'm not trying to pay anybody back. It's just that I'm not Aunty and Uncle's Ryan any more. I'm someone else. Plynlimon changed me. It turned me back into my old self and, if you send me back, I'll never be that self again. There's a Mad Dog Moonlight in me, trying to get out. And, if you don't take me with you, it never will. You've got to take me, or else I'll be Ryan Lewis for ever! Please, *oh please*!'

The sailors put Mad Dog into the taxi. He could see that they weren't happy about it but that they felt they had no choice. Again Phaze II offered to accompany him, but Mad Dog put his hands over his ears.

'You can still be yourself,' Phaze II said, 'wherever you go and whatever happens. You stand and fall by your own efforts in this life, you know. Someone told me that when I was not much older than you, and I've been learning the wisdom of it ever since.'

Mad Dog hated him. He hated his smugness and his stupid words.

'You haven't seen the last of us,' Abren promised. 'We'll come and see you soon. *We promise you.*'

Mad Dog slammed the door in her face. He was fed up with empty promises.

At the last minute, Abren opened the taxi door again and handed something in to him. 'You nearly forgot this,' she said, pressing his *ffon* upon him.

Mad Dog stared at it. '*Where did you get that from?*' he said.

'You brought it with you,' Abren replied.

'No I didn't,' Mad Dog said. 'I didn't bring anything. That's not my *ffon*. Take it away.'

He tried to give it back, but Abren wouldn't have it. 'Of course it's yours. It's certainly not ours,' she said.

'It must be,' Mad Dog said.

'You were waving it at us in the kitchen of No. 3.'

'You're lying.'

'Why would I do that? Why won't you believe me?'

Fuelled by anger, Mad Dog took the cane, broke it in half and threw it back at Abren. 'It's not mine!' he shouted. 'Stop playing games with me!!'

All the way home he raged about people, mountains and even walking canes playing games with him. He was still raging when the taxi driver pulled up outside the hotel. Aunty paid him and he let Mad Dog out, saying to her, 'Rather you than me,' before driving off fast. Aunty tried to get Mad Dog indoors, but he fought like a wild dog being taken into captivity. Uncle came running out to help and Elvis stood in the background, wide-eyed with shock.

'The boy's gone crazy!' Uncle said. 'He needs a doctor to sedate him!'

'He doesn't need sedating,' Aunty said. 'Don't be ridiculous. He's simply overwrought. And exhausted. I mean, look at him. Look at the state of him. All that boy needs is his bed.'

25

Aunty's Birthday

Aunty was right. Getting Mad Dog to bed was difficult, but the minute his head hit the pillow he was asleep. He slept all night and half the next day too, and the first thing he thought about, when he awoke, wasn't what had happened over the last few days. It was his *ffon*.

Mad Dog went to check the wardrobe where it was kept, anxious to prove that it was still there. But, to his horror, it was gone. He searched under the bed. Searched all the other cupboards and drawers. Searched the living room, kitchen and bathroom, and ended up taking the whole vardo apart.

But Abren had been right, it seemed. Mad Dog mightn't understand how the stick she'd given him could have been his *ffon*. But reluctantly he had to admit it was – and then what he'd done to it finally sank in.

'The only thing I've inherited from my past – *and I've broken it in half and thrown it away!*'

When Uncle came to see if Mad Dog was awake, he found him in bed, hidden behind a massive barricade of furniture.

'We've got to talk,' he said, 'so you'd better come out of there. I'll tell your aunty you're awake.'

She left the kitchen to Ruth and Kathleen, and came over straight away. Together she and Uncle put back all the furniture, leaving Mad Dog exposed. Elvis came in from playing, as if he didn't want to miss out.

Mad Dog sat on his bed, watching them getting ready for the big showdown.

'Look, I'm sorry. All right?' he said.

'Oh yes? What for?' Uncle replied. 'Sorry for running off, or sorry for being sent back?'

Mad Dog had never seen Uncle more angry, even when he'd called him a child-thief. He wasn't shouting this time, and he didn't go stomping off, but this was worse somehow. There was something worn about him, as if he'd had enough. *Really* had enough.

'I'm sorry for upsetting you,' Mad Dog said.

'*Upsetting us?*' Uncle said, giving a short laugh. 'Is that what you call it?'

Aunty frowned at him, as if to say *enough*. 'Why did you do it?' she said. 'Why did you go off?'

Mad Dog shrugged.

'Especially after you promised,' Uncle chipped in.

'When did I do that?' Mad Dog said.

'You promised years ago. On the family Bible,' Uncle said.

Mad Dog flared up. 'That's rich,' he said, ignoring Uncle but looking directly at Aunty. 'Am I the only one who breaks their promises? *I think not!*'

Aunty flushed. 'If you're talking about No. 3 –' she began.

'I'm talking about you promising that we'd move back down there in the autumn!' Mad Dog shouted at her, glaring as if to say *get out of that*.

Uncle took a deep breath and said, 'God give me strength!' He also said – slowly so that even a fool would understand it – that sometimes, with the best will in the world, certain promises did have to be broken.

'And the sale of No. 3 is one of those times,' he said. 'It's for your good, although you don't seem to be able to see it. We're not just thinking of ourselves here. If we can find a purchaser for No. 3, then we can afford all the little extras that we don't have at the moment – including building ourselves a family apartment at the back of the hotel.'

'Why do we need that?' Mad Dog said.

'Well, it's obvious. We can't go on for ever working out of a caravan!' Uncle said.

'What's wrong with caravans?' Mad Dog said. He could feel his temper rising to dangerous levels.

'Are you kidding me?' said Uncle. 'The way we're living now we couldn't even swing a cat!'

'Oh, is that right?' Mad Dog said. 'Well, my parents' van wasn't half this size *but it was good enough for us!!*'

He didn't yell, but he didn't have to. Uncle and Aunty stared at him, their surprise obvious because never, in all their years together, had he mentioned anything about his old life.

'You didn't tell us your parents lived in a van,' Aunty said.

'Why should I tell you anything? I don't trust you,' Mad Dog said.

For the rest of the day, he refused to say another thing. He also refused to get off his bed except to go to the toilet and fetch his meals. Every time Aunty came anywhere near him, he glared at her and, when she told him that she loved him, he called her *traitor*.

That night in bed, Mad Dog heard Aunty crying. 'I know, I know,' he heard her say. 'I've brought this on myself. I never should have put No. 3 on the market without discussing it with all of us. You warned me there'd be trouble, but I wouldn't listen. I've done it again, haven't I? Rushed in without thinking. It's what I always do. But what's done is done, and I can't put it right.'

Next morning there were no signs of tears. Uncle drove down to work in Aberystwyth as usual, and Aunty said she'd got a business to run. Elvis went out to play with his friends and Mad Dog got on the PlayStation and zapped aliens as if his life depended upon it.

But a decision hung over them all, and Mad Dog knew it. No. 3 was still for sale, and he spent long hours on his own, wondering what he really wanted and whether it was fair to expect Aunty to rein in her dreams just because of him.

She was good at what she did, and quite plainly loved it. Uncle too. Mad Dog remembered, when they first started out, thinking that they'd stumbled upon their secret selves. Wasn't that exactly what he wanted for himself – and didn't everybody deserve a thing like that?

'Does it really matter where we live?' he asked himself. 'Surely, like Phaze II said, I can be my real self anywhere.'

This was something that he wrestled with for days. When people spoke to him, he didn't answer, but remained as blank as a plain piece of paper. One day Aunty came to him and said, 'Those terrible deep silences that you go into sometimes – what exactly happens? Where do you go?'

Mad Dog shrugged. He knew what she was on about, but didn't want to talk about it. 'Why do you want to know?' he said.

'Because I want to go there too,' Aunty answered. 'I can see you struggling and I want to be there for you. You don't have to do this on your own, you know. I *can* be trusted, no matter what you think. I want to help you – surely you know that?'

For a horrible moment Mad Dog thought she was going to hug him – but then he was saved by Kathleen in the kitchen calling for assistance. After Aunty had gone, though, he thought about what she'd said. Where *did* he go when those terrible deep silences took over? They'd been going on for years now, but he didn't have a clue, if he was honest with himself.

A couple of evenings later, Mad Dog came across Aunty out in the garden stitching labels on to his new school uniform. It was beginning to get dark. Bats were circling the garden and pigeons cooing down in the wood. Mad Dog wished that he could forgive Aunty sufficiently to talk to her, but realised that, even if he could, he wouldn't know quite what to say.

In any case, Uncle got in first. He came across the lawn in high old spirits, busy with secret preparations for Aunty's birthday next day, which was a significant one because it had an 0 in it – though whether there was a 3 in front of it, or a 4, 5 or 6, Mad Dog didn't know.

Aunty called Uncle over and Mad Dog slipped away. Just as he was entering the hotel, he heard Aunty's clear voice carrying across the garden. It wasn't her birthday they were talking about. Once again, it was him.

'I've been telling you for years that there's a story in that boy, waiting to come out,' Aunty was saying.

'And something's happening at long last. I can feel him changing. Feel something stirring up in him. Feel it coming to a head. I want to be there for him, but he doesn't want me. In fact, I think he hates me.'

Next day, being Aunty's birthday, Mad Dog did his best to prove that whatever he felt it wasn't hate. Maybe Aunty's sisters had the same idea, because they all turned up – the entire lot of them, along with an assortment of husbands, boyfriends and all the children, including Luke, Rhys and Hippie. For once they were one big happy family, eating lunch together round a big table laid in the conservatory because the dining room wasn't big enough.

Aunty lapped up all the attention, opening a mountain of presents and looking around at her family as if their being there, after all their fallings-out, was the best present of all. After they'd finished eating, she tried helping to clear up. But her sisters wouldn't let her.

'We'll do that,' they said. 'You're always working. Now's your chance to sit back and relax.'

Aunty did just that. She took a little, unheard-of afternoon nap and awoke expecting to find the hotel falling apart without her. But, when she came out of the vardo, she found a massive picnic hamper being packed into the Range Rover, and the family poring over a series of maps.

'Ah, you're awake at last. Where do you want to go?' the sisters said.

'I don't know what you're talking about,' Aunty replied.

'We're talking about your birthday picnic,' the sisters said.

Aunty started laughing, and everybody else laughed too. 'Are you serious?' Aunty said. 'I can't go off on picnics. I've got a hotel to run.'

Uncle appeared at the kitchen door. 'Ruth and Kathleen say you only get in the way at the best of times,' he said.

'You're lying – they never said that!' Aunty replied.

'Even if he's lying, it's still your birthday, and we can manage without you for one evening,' Ruth and Kathleen said, coming out behind him. 'So, where are you going?'

Aunty thought about it for a moment, then said, 'All right, then, it's Plynlimon. I'd like to have a picnic on Plynlimon.'

Everybody started rushing about, too busy packing the cars to notice Mad Dog standing in a state of shock, his face bright red. Why had Aunty said it. Why Plynlimon? Had she said it for a reason? Or had she said it off the top of her head? All around him, cars were being filled with blankets, cushions, fold-up chairs, barbecue equipment, cricket sets, tennis rackets, towels, swimming gear, maps, water containers, crates of beer – and the birthday cake.

Mad Dog tried to join in, making it look as if he was helping. But his brain was on another planet. 'Do I *have* to go?' he said when all the cars were packed and everyone was ready to go.

'How could you even *ask* that?' Uncle said. 'It's what your aunty wants, and it's her birthday, so of course you do.'

Part V
The Silver River

26

The Designated Campsite

They drove up in convoy. It was a perfect day for picnicking. Mad Dog tried not to think about where they were going, but kept his mind fixed on the smell of ripe blackberries and the sun on his face. When the mountain did come to mind, he told himself it would be different this time. Plynlimon wouldn't do anything weird to him with all these people around. The knack was to stay close to them and not go wandering off.

Occasionally Mad Dog caught glimpses of the sunlit Rheidol, and once he saw a red kite soaring in the bright sunshine – a perfect picture of freedom. They reached Ponterwyd, and Uncle turned on to the main pass road and started snaking up it. He didn't take the Nant y Moch turn, much to Mad Dog's surprise, but took the back route that the Ingram sisters had shown him. This involved so many twists and turns that Aunty, who was meant to be map-reading, threw up her hands in horror and gave up.

'We're lost,' she said.

'You think I don't know what I'm doing?' Uncle said.

'I think the entire family, following after us, *knows* you don't know what you're doing!' Aunty said.

Uncle laughed and said, 'Relax.' He drove them over open moorland, down in deep dark valleys and out again, through forestry commission land densely planted with rows of conifers, beside rivers, up and down tiny switchback roads, and along lanes so unused that grass grew up the middle of them.

Finally, when Aunty declared that she'd given up all hope of their ever stopping before it got dark, Uncle pulled off the road into an official designated campsite, complete with Welsh and European flags, public lavatories, tourist information boards, taps of running water and way-marked nature trails.

The place was as unexpected as it was unlikely. What all these amenities were doing in a remote corner of Plynlimon, Mad Dog couldn't imagine. Tentatively he got out of the car. There was an area for tents and camper vans on one side of him, set back between trees, and a picturesque view down to a riverbank on the other, with picnic tables, a place for making barbecues and a covered shelter in case of rain.

This was an entirely different Plynlimon to the one that Mad Dog had seen before – and he felt relieved. Telling himself that nothing strange could ever happen in a place like this, he trailed down to the river, which turned out, according to a way-marked sign, to be the Hafren, also known as the Severn.

Uncle called him to come back and help, but he pretended he hadn't heard, and so did all the other Lewis and Williams children, including Luke, Rhys and Hippie. The river was shallow enough to play in, and they charged in without stopping to take off their shoes and proceeded to kick water in each other's faces, laughing and shrieking and running about. In just a few days' time their new big school would claim them. But, just for now, they could lark about and still be little kids.

Finally they trailed back to the picnic site, wet and shivering, hoping that their mothers had thought to bring changes of clothes. Here they found a campfire built and Aunty's sisters cooking over it while she sat with her feet up, doing nothing, as befit the birthday girl. The sun was lowering and the day was golden and mellow. They crouched around the fire to eat food on plastic plates, drink Aunty's health and watch her blow out the candles on her cake. Then one of the sisters' boyfriends got out a guitar and they all started singing.

Aunty sat back, full and contented, her family around her just like in the old days before the Aged Relative's inheritance had become their poisoned chalice. It was beginning to get dark by now, and someone said what a shame it was that they'd have to go. But then, a beer or two later, someone else said, 'Who *says we should go*?' and suddenly the talk was all of how many blankets they'd got between them and whether, with the help of coats and cushions, they could make themselves comfortable for a night under the stars.

It wasn't what they'd planned, but everyone agreed that it was the sort of opportunity that, when it came along, had to be seized. Someone poked the fire and set it sparking. Someone else went off for a fresh supply of wood to see them through the night. The beers went round again, by which time nobody was fit to drive anyway.

Soon half the family was asleep, lulled by fire and song. Mad Dog watched them dropping off one after another. The last to go was Aunty.

'This has been the best birthday ever,' she said.

'Shame I had to get to forty before it happened. But, now it has, I don't want the day to end.'

'I don't either,' Mad Dog said. 'I wasn't sure to begin with, but I'm glad I came.'

'You do know, don't you, that if ever you wanted to talk …' Aunty began.

'… that you'd be there for me,' Mad Dog said.

They both laughed. Aunty said she knew what a pain it must be having someone like her always trying to get inside his head. Mad Dog said he wished that she could. If he could make it happen, he would. In fact, if he could get inside his own head he'd make that happen too.

But Aunty never heard him. Her eyes had proved too heavy and she'd fallen asleep. Mad Dog smiled and pulled a blanket over her. Then he reached for another one, rolled up in front of the fire and tried to sleep as well.

But it wasn't as easy as it looked. Everybody else had dropped off, even Luke, who'd sworn he was going to stay awake all night. Mad Dog itched with restlessness, tossing and turning until he couldn't bear it any more. The harder he tried to sleep, the more awake he felt. What was the matter with him?

In the end, he got up, built up the fire and walked around the campsite. Even in the darkness, it was surprising how much he could see. With nothing but firelight to help him, he could even read the information boards.

They told him nothing he didn't know already from his project at school, but he read them anyway, mugging up on kingfishers and otters, mountain ponies and foxes. He read up on snakes, and how to recognise their different skins. Read up on skylarks and their nesting habits. Memorised wild orchids and which toadstools not to touch.

This was the real Plynlimon, wasn't it? The mountain on these information boards was a world away from washrooms, tarmac car parks and shelters from the rain. And suddenly Mad Dog wanted it again. He wanted cotton-grass and gadflies, ponds full of lilies and mountain springs bursting out of secret places. They were out there, and he felt them calling him.

Mad Dog drew in his breath. He stood there trembling, not quite understanding what was happening to him. Then, behind him, Aunty stirred and the spell was broken. Twice the mountain had lured him away, but not this time.

This time he had more sense.

27

It's Time

Long after the fire had burned out, Mad Dog heard dogs barking. No one else heard them, only him. No one else sat up, took a quick look around to check that everything was all right, then drifted off to sleep only to awaken later as if an alarm clock had gone off inside their head, shrilling the words *it's time*.

Mad Dog sat up like a shot, wanting to believe that he'd dreamt those words but knowing he'd really heard them. He tried to go back to sleep, but something inside his head shouted that it wasn't for sleep that he'd been brought back here to Plynlimon. It wasn't for pretending he hadn't heard things when he had.

Mad Dog got up, knowing he had no choice. This wasn't a matter of staying close to Aunty and keeping safe. It was a matter of doing what he had to. He crept away, telling himself that if there was any reason for his being here, it wasn't for staying wrapped up in blankets, but for following whatever had called him and seeing where it led.

Stepping over Aunty, Mad Dog disappeared into the night. 'You won't even know I did this,' he whispered. 'I'll be back before you wake up.'

Then he was gone, taking the way-marked path down to the river, before following the river up through the forest, heading for its source. Somewhere up there, he told himself, high on Plynlimon in the wild places where the snakes and the red kites lived, was the one thing he was looking for. The mystery. The treasure. The answer to his questions. Whatever.

Mad Dog walked through the darkness and never felt lost. Every other time on Plynlimon, its vastness had overwhelmed him. But, this time, every tree he passed and every twist and turn along the riverbank felt like an old friend. Climbing Plynlimon felt as easy as walking round his own garden.

Eventually the forest fell behind Mad Dog. He scrambled over a stile and found himself on the open mountaintop. The night was cloudy, not a star in sight. But he didn't need starlight to know where he was. He could smell the mountain all around him, peaty and alive.

Mad Dog walked for miles across the silent grasslands. At one point, he found himself at the *ffynnon* of the Severn, surrounded by a sea of duckboards. He stopped to look at the little bit of black bog, clogged with lichen, that marked its source, marvelling that this could be the start of anything big enough to become so mighty a river. Then he carried on, passing close to the Wye's source too, though not stopping to look for it because the words *it's time* drew him on.

But time for what? Mad Dog didn't know. All he knew was that the night seemed to go on for ever, day never breaking and the sky never getting any lighter. On the far side of Plynlimon, he picked his way down a tricky little rocky gully, not knowing where it was leading but feeling perfectly at home – and that even before he saw the van.

It was in the bottom of the valley – a broken-down,

rusty thing, crouching like a dead beast on the side of the track. At first Mad Dog assumed that it was empty and abandoned, but then the smell of wood smoke came his way and he looked again and noticed a thin strand of smoke winding out of a tin-can chimney.

Immediately Mad Dog's heart started turning like a piston. He knew that smell of wood smoke, didn't he? And he knew that chimney too. In fact, he even knew that van – and a long, low breath came whistling out of him like a train out of a tunnel. Of course he knew that van! There were curtains at the windows, and he knew those curtains. And he knew the lights behind those curtains.

They were the lights of home!

Mad Dog cried out loud. No wonder Plynlimon had felt like his back garden! It *was* his back garden. At least, it had been all those years ago!

He started running. Someone inside the van must have heard him because a door opened. A woman appeared in a handful of yellow light. She had long hair, a flowing skirt, a tea towel in one hand and a baby in the other.

She was Mad Dog's mother.

His mother!

Mad Dog stumbled towards her. Strange sounds came out of his throat, meant to be words but completely indecipherable. Mad Dog's mother waved to him, but she didn't come to greet him. Instead, in measured tones – as if he'd only just stepped out to play and this was just another ordinary day – she called, 'There you are. I was just wondering how long you'd be. Supper's on the table. Come and eat.'

Mad Dog wanted to hug her, but she'd already

turned back inside. In a state of confusion, he followed her, only to find his dad, of all people – his dad, *his dad!* – sat perched on an all-too-familiar bench at a tiny, all-too-familiar, fold-up table. When he saw Mad Dog, he showed not a flicker of surprise. He didn't hug him or get up. He didn't even scold him or ask where he'd been. And as for how much he'd grown – neither he nor Mad Dog's mother made a single comment.

'You'd better wash before you eat. Your hands are filthy,' was all that either of them said.

Mad Dog couldn't work it out. None of it made sense. What was going on here? Where were his mother's tears? Why didn't his dad want to know where he'd been? What was wrong with his parents – and *who was that baby?*

When Mad Dog had washed his hands, his dad made room for him on the bench. There they were, all together again for the first time in years, and Mad Dog mightn't have been away at all. Never once, in all his dreams of finding his parents, had he imagined it would be like this. His parents looked unchanged by the years, as did the van. But he had changed, and he wanted everybody to comment on how big he was, how tall and grown up, what a different boy from the one who went away.

Instead, Mad Dog's parents carried on as if nothing much had happened since he'd gone. His dad went on about some problem to do with the van's engine, which would cost a fortune to repair. His mum went on about the baby. She didn't ask about Elvis. Maybe one baby was much like any other as far as she was concerned. Maybe Elvis was forgotten and she didn't miss him, just as she obviously hadn't missed Mad Dog.

After supper, Mad Dog's mother folded up the table and his dad pulled down their beds. The little fold-down cot, which had once been Elvis's, now belonged to this new baby, but Mad Dog's bed was still his own. He expected it to be too small for him but, when he climbed in, he found that it fitted perfectly.

His mother tucked him in as if he was still a five-year-old, then, taking a coat off the back of the door, she went and sat on the step to give the baby its final feed. Mad Dog's dad went and sat with her, and Mad Dog was left alone.

He lay looking around the van, marvelling that everything – every last, single thing – was exactly the same. You'd have thought there'd been some changes, but even the same bucket stood in for a sink. The kitchen cupboards were just the same, showing off his dad's carpentry skills. And the exact same bits of silver jewellery were scattered about everywhere, made by Mad Dog's mother.

Mad Dog fell asleep at last, comforted by the sameness of it all. But when he awoke later he found that his parents still hadn't come to bed, but that the step was empty.

Mad Dog called, but no one replied. He went and stood on the step, but couldn't see a soul outside and a sense of panic washed over him. Surely he couldn't have found his parents again, only to lose them! What sort of carelessness was that?

Mad Dog called again. Still no one replied, but this time, somewhere off in the darkness, he caught a sound of singing. A sense of relief washed over him.

Singing, he told himself. Only singing – and how many times had his dad gone off in the night to sing to himself beneath the stars? There was nothing to worry about here. All that had happened was that his mother had gone with him, taking the baby.

But the sense of having nearly lost something was hard to shake off. Mad Dog started following the singing, anxious to rejoin his family. The stony track outside the van led him up a small hillock from which he could see a campfire down the other side. He couldn't see his parents, but he could hear his father singing and his mother laughing.

Mad Dog started down the track, trying not to feel resentful because his parents had taken the baby but left him behind. By the time he got anywhere near the campfire, which had been built against the side of a broken-down old wall, the baby was crying but neither parent was doing anything about it. They were too busy having a good time, sharing from a bottle that Mad Dog could see them passing back and forth between each other.

It wasn't like Mad Dog's parents to ignore a crying baby, and he found himself surprised. His mother in particular had always been so caring around Elvis. She'd had her grouchy moments – especially when she was tired – but she'd always been there for him. Always treated him with tenderness. Always been so quick to sense her baby's needs.

So what was going on here? Why was Mad Dog's mother ignoring this new baby? And why was she acting so differently to her normal self? As Mad Dog watched, she staggered to her feet, shaking with laughter as if something was hysterically funny. Mad

Dog couldn't see anything to laugh about, but she swayed from side to side, unable to stand straight.

What was the matter with her? Mad Dog's mother had never been the sort of person to laugh at nothing, and she'd had no time for people who did. Even if a thing was funny, it was hard to get her laughing, though sometimes Mad Dog's father had succeeded, cracking a joke that was so terrible that she'd throw back her head and it would be as if all the light of the world was pouring out of her.

But she wasn't laughing like that now. It wasn't light coming out of her. It was something else. Mad Dog reached the wall, which he now realised was the remains of a ruined cottage, and peered round the edge of it. Something was wrong with his mother – wrong with both his parents. A steady stream of bottles was passing between them, getting drained and being thrown away, glass smashing everywhere. He could never remember his parents acting like that before. Never remember them throwing rubbish around, never remember them being even tipsy. But now his mother's head was lolling this way and that, and her long hair was flying, and his dad was crouching at her side, half-dancing, half-stamping like an enraged beast.

Why were they behaving like that? Before tonight, his mother had never been anything less than graceful, but now she shook like a tree in a storm, all flailing branches and flying limbs. She had something in her hand and was trying to do some sort of little drum majorette's routine with it, throwing it up into the air in a twist of silver and laughing hysterically when she failed to catch it. One time it fell in the fire and her skirt almost caught alight when she scrambled to retrieve it.

Mad Dog cried out, but his mother didn't hear him and neither did his dad. He'd snatched the thing out of the fire and was teasing Mad Dog's mother with it, whirling it around and holding her out of reach. She kept leaping up and trying to get it, but he broke away from her and started staggering down the track with her following him, shouting *give that here*.

Mad Dog watched them and didn't know which he should do – take the baby and return to the van where he could pretend he'd never seen any of this happen, or go after his parents and try to get them to behave like their old selves. In the end, he chose the latter course.

Promising the baby that he'd be back, he stumbled downhill following the track. Here, right in the bottom of the valley, he found a river flowing through the darkness and his dad ankle-deep in it, bottles in each hand. His mother was in it too, trying again with her drum majorette routine. She'd regained whatever it was she'd been fighting for, and was tossing it up in the air and catching it while his father tried to get it off her. The two of them were laughing, wading out deeper, swigging from the bottles and throwing them about.

Mad Dog followed them to the water's edge, knowing that he had to do something before his parents got themselves into serious trouble. His mother was up to her waist by now, shivering and shrieking. Mad Dog yelled at her to come back, but she didn't hear and neither did his dad, too busy splashing her and horsing around.

Mad Dog yelled again, only this time louder. 'Mother! Dadda! Stop it! *Stop it! STOP IT!!*'

Mad Dog started wading out as well, but his parents didn't notice him. They were right out in the middle of the river now, holding each other tight and swirling round and round. Mad Dog's mother's hair flew round her like a cloud of darkness. It flew round them both. Then she threw up what Mad Dog now saw was a stick – and lost her footing in the process, and started keeling over.

After that, everything happened at extraordinary speed. Mad Dog's dad grabbed his mother, but then lost his footing too, and the two of them went down like a pair of pins in a bowling alley. They were there one second and gone the next, leaving nothing but a walking cane, which came falling out of the sky for Mad Dog to catch.

He was reaching out for his parents, but his *ffon* fell into his hands instead! Not that he realised what it was. He was far too busy trying to find his parents. By now he was out in the middle of the river as well, but he couldn't see them anywhere. He was up to his chest and the river's undercurrent was dragging at his feet, trying to tip him over.

Mad Dog stumbled in a panic, looking for a better footing. For a moment he nearly tumbled headlong like his parents had done. But then, thanks to the *ffon*, he managed to regain his balance. He felt it take his weight, felt the familiar silver topknot beneath his fist. Looked down and there it was, steadying him and saving his life.

But any questions about how it had got there had to be put aside for later. For even as Mad Dog struggled out of the water, a figure caught his attention. He was standing on a stony bank, his arms full of bottles, watching everything that was going on. At first Mad Dog thought he was his dad, who had struggled ashore. But his dad was dark, whereas this figure had goldish-coloured hair and was the taller of the two. And he wasn't wet as if he'd just come out of a river, and his face belonged to a stranger. It might be night-time, and the man might be wrapped about in shadows, but Mad Dog knew he wasn't his dad.

The important thing, though, was that help was at hand. 'Here, quickly! *Help!*' Mad Dog cried, wading towards the figure.

But, instead of helping, the stranger burst out laughing. Mad Dog reeled back as if he'd been slapped. The man threw back his head. His eyes danced like twin fires with malevolent intent – and there was something about those eyes. Something about that laugh. Something strangely familiar.

Before Mad Dog could figure out what, however, a din broke out around him that sounded like the howl of dogs but grew until Mad Dog felt as if an entire mountain was raining down on him. Behind him, he heard the river crying as if it wanted no part in what was going on. But already it was too late. Darkness fell, and the sky fell with it, and Mad Dog was overwhelmed. The river rose as if it had no choice and Mad Dog's last thought, as his feet were swept out from under him, was that everything had been for this.

The words *it's time* had been for this.

Everything he'd done in his whole life had been for this.

This moment now.

Everything had brought him here.

When Mad Dog came to, he found that he'd been washed up by the river and deposited face-down on a grassy bank. He lay there, shivering but alive, knowing that the Rheidol had rescued him. He could have drowned, but it hadn't let him. The one river that ran through his life – it had saved him from death.

But what about his parents? Where was their rescue? Mad Dog struggled to his feet, but he knew he wouldn't see them, because everything felt different now. The world had changed. It felt a smaller place.

Once the night had rung with songs and laughter, but now it was filled with the most terrible deep silence. And it was the silence that had lain inside Mad Dog for all these years. Every time when Aunty had asked him where he went, then this was it. *This night from his childhood, which he'd just lived through again!*

Mad Dog searched the river until morning, and never found his parents. Finally the sun appeared over Plynlimon Fawr and an all-too-familiar-looking cross-roads between valleys emerged into the light. Mad Dog recognised it immediately, and he recognised the ruined cottage beside the track and understood why he'd been so frightened standing on that hillock, scared to take another step.

On the way back to the van, Mad Dog passed the remains of the campfire that his parents had sat around on the last night of their lives. The whole thing felt like years ago now, not something that had happened only last night. The van too, when he climbed over the hillock and found it on the other side, looked as if it had been abandoned for years. Its roof had half caved in, its windows hung off their frames, its curtains were in tatters and most of its fittings had weathered to the point of rotting.

Looking down upon his little narrow bed, its mattress shredded and its springs sticking out, Mad Dog understood that the past was back where it was meant to be – in the past – and the time had come to move on.

'It's what I never did,' he said out loud. 'Somewhere deep inside myself, I was always here. When I lost my parents, my body walked away but my Mad Dog self remained. That's why I could never explain where I came from, when people asked. Because the real me was still here, and the boy that they were talking to was just a shell.'

Mad Dog left the van as he had left it once before, years ago when he'd lost his parents and hadn't known what else to do. Somewhere on the other side of Plynlimon, he told himself, lay a world where the worst that could happen was a house going up for sale without anybody asking. In that world, mountains didn't fall like shadows, parents didn't dance themselves to death and mysterious strangers didn't stand in the darkness, refusing to help and laughing at their predicament.

Mad Dog walked all day. Sometimes he stopped and ate blackberries, cramming his mouth full of them. Sometimes he drank from mountain springs. Occasionally he stopped to rest, though never for long, in case exhaustion got him and he fell into the sort of sleep from which he wouldn't wake. People went up Plynlimon, after all, and never came back, and Mad Dog didn't want to be one of them.

Finally, in the late afternoon, he found what he was looking for – or, to be more precise, *she* found him. Lost in woodland, contemplating yet another night out in the open, Mad Dog heard a sound in the undergrowth somewhere up ahead. For a moment he thought it was a fox or snake or otter. But then a figure appeared between the trees, and the next thing he knew, it was running towards him.

It was Aunty. *Aunty*, with her arms outstretched and Uncle behind her, crying out with relief. Mad Dog ran towards them and they scooped him up. This time there was no scolding for running away. Tears poured down Mad Dog's cheeks. They poured down Aunty's too, and she hugged him hard. Then Uncle hugged him and said something about Elvis.

Exhausted and confused, Mad Dog started panicking. 'The baby!' he cried out. *'The baby...! Where's the baby? I forgot the baby. I promised I'd go back for it, and I never did ...'*

He didn't stop until Elvis appeared. His baby brother Elvis, a schoolboy now and all grown up. And if Mad Dog had any doubts that the past was back where it was meant to be, he only had to stand there while his brother flung his arms around his neck.

28

Mad Dog, Mad Dog, Mad Dog

Back in the vardo, his head on his pillow and his eyes refusing to stay open, Mad Dog knew that he'd come home. These people were his family now. As much as any of those names in Aunty's big family Bible, he was one of them. Through the thin bedroom wall, he could hear Aunty and Uncle talking about what had happened, trying to reassure each other that some sort of watershed had been crossed and nothing like this would ever happen again. Poor old them, Mad Dog thought. What he'd put them through. Poor old Aunty and Uncle and Elvis, not to say anything of his friends. Hippie … Luke … Rhys …

Mad Dog fell asleep. When he awoke, the rest of the day had passed and it was getting dark. He opened his eyes. Uncle was leaning over him and slowly he realised that he was shaking him awake.

'Ryan, Ryan,' he was saying. 'Get dressed. Come on. You've got visitors.'

Mad Dog pulled on his clothes and went out to the living room – only to find the sailors, Abren and Phaze II, being fussed over by Aunty. *The sailors!* Mad Dog stood in the doorway. Aunty was going on about coincidences but Mad Dog knew that, where the sailors were concerned, nothing ever happened by accident.

When she saw him, Abren rose to her feet. 'Good to see you,' she said, a smile on her face. 'We've brought you something. You've probably been missing it, and it's *definitely* been missing you. This is going to sound crazy, but it wants you back. We were driven here by it. Sitting there in the boat, it made us come. Tomorrow wouldn't have done. All the way up from Aberystwyth, it had to be today.'

She raised a hand in which she held a miraculously restored *ffon*, only the slightest mark bearing witness to what Mad Dog had done to it. He took it from her, feeling its weight of history. This was the *ffon* that he'd broken in a temper, but it was also the *ffon* that had saved him in the river. The one his mother had thrown up into the air as she'd keeled over, and he had caught. And never again would he wonder how it had come into his possession, because now he knew.

'Thank you,' he said.

Aunty insisted that the sailors should stay overnight and be her guests. It was getting late, she said, and she wouldn't dream of them turning round and driving all the way back to Aberystwyth. She installed them in the best room in the hotel, which she somehow, mysteriously, managed to make vacant. Any bitterness she'd ever felt about the way they'd once sneaked off, years ago without goodbyes, was forgotten. Now that she knew it was they who'd looked after Mad Dog and taxied him home when they'd found him in the Gap, there wasn't anything she wouldn't do for them.

Mad Dog left them heading for the dining room to be fed like kings, and went and sat out on the vardo step. Here he looked out over the garden and listened to Uncle getting Elvis ready for bed. It was the music of home, and it sounded good.

Up above him the moon rose. All around him the

night was gentle and still, warm and safe. Mad Dog pulled the *ffon* towards him, feeling as if he'd reached journey's end. His story was complete. Everything he needed to know had been found out. Everything that needed to be done had been accomplished.

Silently he nursed his *ffon*, drawing strength from it in ways he'd never understood before. Its silver topknot glowed in the moonlight, its intricately engraved swirls looking almost fluid, like the currents running through a river. Mad Dog remembered what Grendel had said about it shining in the long grass. He remembered what she'd said about its light and he'd thought she'd made it up. But it *did* have a light.

Mad Dog tipped the topknot towards him, running his fingers over its letters and catching them in the light. It was as if the cane was speaking to him, explaining that he'd got it wrong and his story wasn't over yet, not quite.

Slowly, curiously, Mad Dog ran his fingers over the engraved curls that made up the W, then followed the outline of the A, then traced the imprint of the fancy Os that were so intricate he scarcely could believe that human hands had made them. Finally he traced the letter at the end, which he'd always thought of as a C for 'cat' but, he now realised with some surprise, looked more like a G for 'God'.

Mad Dog held the topknot close, wondering if, when he'd thrown the *ffon* at Abren, it had got damaged. There were no dents that he could see, not even any scratches. But the letter was definitely a G and, if he'd ever thought otherwise, then he'd been reading it wrong.

Mad Dog ran his fingers back over the letters,

checking for other mistakes. He reached the middle Os, and probed behind them, lifting them close again. Suddenly it came to him that they weren't the same. The second was an O, most definitely, but the first looked more like a D, or even two Ds, looped inseparably around each other.

Mad Dog sucked in his breath. Instead of spelling out W-A-O-O-C, as he'd always thought, the word now spelled out W-A-D-D-O-G, or WAD DOG! Or even, if he'd got it wrong about the W –

'MAD DOG!'

Mad Dog said the words out loud, and a thrill, as powerful as electricity, ran through him. What was it his father had once said about the *ffon* being there for him when he grew up *and wanted to know who he was*?

'This is it,' he whispered, staring at the word. 'Who I am, spelt out for me! I can't believe it, and yet it's true. All these years it was *my name* that followed me around and never let me go, always close to hand though I never knew! It was *my name* that made me feel so safe! That's what lit up the darkness when Grendel found it on the mountain. And, in that river, when I nearly got swept away, it was *my name* that steadied me and saved my life!'

He started laughing. It was the simply best laugh of his life, open and pure, with nothing to taint it. He had cracked it at last. The secret code he'd struggled to decipher. The mystery he'd tried so hard to fathom. It wasn't just a bunch of letters, after all. It had a meaning, and he knew what it was.

It was *himself*.

He was its meaning.

He, *Mad Dog*.

Uncle called, 'You all right out there?' and Mad Dog called back that he was, oh, yes, he was! He got down from the vardo step, too overwhelmed to stay still, and started walking about the garden, swinging his *ffon* and feeling his name beneath his hand. Once he'd thought that there were mysteries in life that went deeper than words, but now he knew that nothing could go deeper than the right word understood at exactly the right moment.

Mad Dog did a victor's lap around the hotel grounds, starting with the lawn that ran down to the road, then crossing the front of the hotel where the guests ate out in the evenings, and then slipping down the side of the building, passing the conservatory on the way, and cutting round the back between the kitchen and the one reminder of the Aged Relative's old B & B that Aunty had never been able to get rid of – the dripping cliff.

'You all right?' called the kitchen ladies as Mad Dog bumped into them, pulling on their jackets, ready to head home.

'I'm fine,' Mad Dog called back. 'Couldn't be better.'

Ruth turned out the light, and Kathleen closed the kitchen door and said, 'Well, goodnight then.' They headed for the car park and were quickly gone.

Mad Dog listened to the sound of their cars fading and watched their lights disappearing. The garden was quiet again, and the night smelt sweet and musky. An owl called from a tree off in the wood somewhere. A little breeze rustled along the ground and Mad Dog shivered at the sound of it. Suddenly he felt lonely out there in the darkness without Aunty, Uncle, Elvis and the sailors. His lap of honour was over and, wanting home, he turned back to the vardo.

'*So, Mad Dog is it?*' a voice said.

Mad Dog spun round. At first he couldn't see anything, just the back of the hotel and the cliff half-hidden in shadows and glistening with moisture. But then something moved among those shadows, rippling like curtains on a stage before the beginning of a performance when the players are behind it, ready to begin.

'Who's there?' Mad Dog said.

For a moment, no one answered. Then the shadows parted and a figure materialised, followed by a pack of huge, pale dogs. His face was grey and drawn, his eyes as black as wrinkled prunes and he had red tattoos all over his chest. His presence seemed to fill the space between the kitchen and the cliff. Mad Dog caught a glimpse of silver charms around his neck, and knew that he should run.

'*It's you,*' he said.

The Manager's smile was tight and cruel. 'And it's *you*,' he replied. 'Little Ryan Lewis – who thought he had a secret message passed down by his parents, but it turned out just to be a name! And what a name! I mean, *Mad Dog*! What sort of name is that?'

He laughed, and Mad Dog shivered. He gripped his *ffon* but he could feel all his pride in his name and who he was slipping away.

'Life's full of disappointments, isn't it?' the Manager said. 'Secrets that aren't secret after all. Codes that tell you nothing you don't already know. Who'd have thought it? The things you put your hopes in always let you down. Take parents, for example. One moment they're all over you – the best parents in the world with stars in their eyes and your life in their hands – and, the next, they're drunk and in the river, and you're all alone and fending for yourself. What sort of life is that?'

He laughed again. Threw back his head and laughed – and Mad Dog knew where he'd heard that laugh before.

'It was *you*,' he said. 'You last night when I went back in time. It was you I called to for help, but you wouldn't come. You standing on the shore with your armful of bottles. You who got my parents drunk. Got them dancing. Put a spell on them and made them fool about. You who drove them out into the river, and watched them lose their footing and didn't care. But *why*? What did they ever do to you? I don't understand. Who *are* you?'

The Manager didn't answer. Instead he took a step towards Mad Dog. His eyes were blacker than ever, and if his tattoos looked any redder they'd have burnt up the night. Mad Dog knew that he should be calling for Uncle, Aunty, the sailors – anybody – because he'd never get another chance.

The Manager smiled. He said that, even if Mad Dog did call, people were never there when you needed them. Didn't he know that?

'However full your life may seem, you're always really alone,' the Manager said. 'And when I say *alone*, this is what I mean …'

Leaning forward, he removed the *ffon* from under Mad Dog's arm as easily as taking candy from a baby, then threw it up into the air – and suddenly it wasn't there any more. It didn't come down again. It simply disappeared, as if the Manager had conjured it out of existence. And, in its moment of disappearance, Mad Dog suddenly felt as if he too had been conjured out of existence.

'*What've you done?*' he gasped.

The Manager laughed. Mad Dog tried to back away from him, but the Manager looked into him with his huge black eyes and Mad Dog felt aloneness soaking into him. In the Manager's eyes, he could see himself reflected – a pathetic little scrap of a boy who didn't even have it in him to save a walking cane, let alone his parents when they'd needed him!

For, if his parents were dead, *it was all Mad Dog's fault*! When they'd been drowning, he'd been floundering about. And, when they'd been swept away, he'd been saving himself. Instead of drawing on his Trojan blood and performing acts of heroism, he'd been out cold, lying on the riverbank. It wasn't because of the Manager that his parents were dead.

It was because of him.

The Manager laughed as if he knew exactly what Mad Dog was thinking. His eyes bored into Mad Dog's, and he felt himself shrinking. He was glad his *ffon* had gone, because he didn't deserve it and he certainly didn't deserve the name on it. Even Ryan Lewis was too good a name for him. And, as for Mad Dog Moonlight – it was light years beyond what he was worth.

Mad Dog shrank before the Manager's gaze. As the light and life went out of him, he could sense the Manager growing. It was almost as if he was feeding on him. His silver necklace gleamed upon his tattooed chest, which seemed to be growing all the time. Everything about him seemed to be growing, from the hands that gripped Mad Dog to the lines on his tattoos – and there was nothing Mad Dog could do to stop it happening.

He was getting weaker by the minute, everything that made him unique and special coming out. And the Manager was doing it to him, but he didn't know how. First the newly regained memory of his parents came out, then the memory of his brother Elvis. Then his homes came out, both the vardo and No. 3, then all his memories of Aunty and Uncle. Then the sailors came out, and then Mad Dog's friends.

And then even Mad Dog's feelings came out – every last moment of happiness, sadness, tears and joy, as if he'd never had them. And his past, present and future came out with them, and then even his name.

Mad Dog's name – for God's sake, even that! Once he'd had a *ffon* to keep it safe for him, but now he couldn't even remember what it was!

Mad Dog felt what little fight was left in him go out like a light. There might be only one story running through his life, but it had run to its end. The little baby who'd howled because he'd missed seeing a silver river in the sky, and whose mother had said, '*Don't you ever let anybody take your name from you, because it's who you are,*' was dead and gone, and there was nothing Mad Dog could do to bring him back.

The Manager laughed as if he knew that, in this battle of his making, he had won. Mad Dog reached out – but felt nothing there. For a moment he teetered on the brink of darkness. But then, deep within himself, something started rising.

Mad Dog felt it in his gut and he felt it in his heart. It rose in his bones and it rose in his blood. He heard it in his lungs, rising like a howl, and he heard it in his brain. And, like a massive flood, the howl came spilling out.

The sheer force of it drove back the Manager as if before the waters of a mighty flood. Mad Dog slipped from his grasp and there was nothing that could be done to stop it happening. Mad Dog felt himself break free, but that didn't stop him howling. *This is who I am*, the howl seemed to say. *This is how it is*, and the Manager couldn't stand against it. He couldn't bear it. He didn't stand a chance.

Suddenly, like a storm that had spent its force, the Manager went hurtling back into the shadows of the cliff, and his dogs went hurtling after him, and the darkness closed around them and they were gone.

But, even afterwards, standing there alone between the kitchen and the cliff, Mad Dog howled on and on. He didn't need the Manager to tell him his name. Didn't need his mother. Didn't even need a walking cane. So what if it was gone! He knew who he was. It was engraved in his bones. It was engraved in his blood.

'WAOOC!' he howled. 'WADDOG! MADDOG! MAD DOG! *MAD DOG! MAD DOG!!!*'

29

The Title Deeds of Plynlimon Mountain

Long before Mad Dog finished yelling, half the hotel had come rushing to see what was wrong, including Aunty, Uncle and Elvis. Aunty reassured them all that there was nothing to see, just a boy having a tantrum, and ushered them away. But the sailors refused to be ushered away. They came flying to Mad Dog's side and closed ranks round him as if – even though they hadn't been there to witness it – they understood what was going on.

He was safe now, they assured Mad Dog. They were there and nothing could get him. Three were stronger than one – stronger by far, but it was over, anyway.

Over. Safe. They repeated the words loudly to make sure he could hear. But, as if terrified of forgetting again, Mad Dog couldn't stop calling out his name. It flowed out of him like a river. Mad Dog … Mad Dog … Mad Dog … On and on it flowed until his voice gave out. And, even then, he wouldn't stop, whispering, '*Mad Dog … Mad Dog … Mad Dog …*'

Nobody quite knew what to do. Uncle tried coaxing Mad Dog back towards the vardo, but got pushed away. Aunty tried to hold him, but got pushed away as well. For the first time ever, she conceded that maybe a doctor would have to get involved. She was out of her depth, she said – and it wasn't often that Aunty admitted to anything like that.

'Leave this to us,' said Phaze II. 'You won't need doctors. We can sort this out.'

'We understand what's going on, because we've been here too,' said Abren. 'Trust us.'

And that's what Aunty and Uncle did. Maybe, at some deep level, they understood that the sailors hadn't just turned up tonight to return a stick, but for this as well. Or maybe they trusted them because they knew they had no choice. But, either way, they ushered a frightened and crying Elvis back into the vardo, and closed the door, calling to the sailors, 'You know where we are.'

After that, the night became very still, as if holding its breath. The lights in the hotel went out, then they went out in the vardo and still the sailors stood on either side of Mad Dog, never asking anything, never saying anything, simply being there.

Finally Mad Dog stopped shaking and his name stopped leaking out of him. He looked up at the sailors, as if seeing them for the first time.

'You told me once that some people leave Plynlimon but never really get away,' he croaked. 'I didn't know then what you meant – but I do now. It's *him*, isn't it? The Manager. He's the one you can't get away from. But who is he?'

The sailors glanced at each other as if this was the one question, above all others, that they'd been waiting for, not knowing quite how they were going to answer it. Then Abren took a deep breath and said, 'It would be easy to tell you that he's some high elf-lord out of a book – the Red Judge of Plynlimon, or someone like that, and his dogs the *cŵn y wbir*, the legendary Dogs of the Sky ...'

'Easy to tell you that he's any of the other names that people have for him,' Phaze II joined in. 'And there are plenty of them, believe me – king of conjurors, tricky trickster, king of thieves, mountain man – you name it, he's been called it ...'

'But, underneath the names that people have for him,' Abren added, 'there's more to it than that. There are truths behind old stories that people rarely see. And the truth behind your Manager is that he's not that different to you and me. He may be every nightmare that we ever dreamt. But, beyond the lies that roll so easily off his tongue, beyond the cruelty, beyond the games for power and control, is a living, breathing being with hopes and fears, people that he loved once, people that he lost, choices he made and choices that he could have made but never did. And what he is we could all become, sucked in without a whimper – unless we do what you've just done.'

'And what's that?' Mad Dog whispered, scarcely daring to speak out loud.

'Make a stand. Be yourself. Nothing else will do,' Abren said.

She shivered. Mad Dog shivered too. There were things here that he didn't understand, and maybe never would. Words like *king of conjurors* and *Red Judge of Plynlimon* whirled about his head, but suddenly he could feel autumn blowing up the garden and he found himself prepared to let them go. Another time, he thought. He could think about them then. Think about the Manager, and what he'd done, and about himself and what he'd done as well, defeating him with nothing but a name.

But, just for now, all Mad Dog wanted was

ordinary life again – not this talk of living, breathing beings and the choices that they made, but supper and his bed.

'Let's go inside,' he said.

The sailors said that was a good idea and turned towards the vardo. Before they could get to it, however, a long, wispy sheet of what looked like paper came blowing along the ground between the kitchen and the cliff. Mad Dog stooped to pick it up, and saw that it was covered in red lines. He didn't know what it was but, at the sight of those lines, he shivered and took an instinctive backwards step.

'What have you got there?' Abren said.

Phaze II picked up the paper. Abren said she thought it was a map. Phaze II said he knew a thing or two about maps and it wasn't like any map he'd ever seen. Mad Dog agreed, but Abren insisted that she was right. Look. Here. She'd found the River Severn, she said. Her river, she called it. And then Phaze II pointed out what he thought might be the Wye, and perhaps they both were right because suddenly Mad Dog started seeing things too – roads and contours, woods and villages, towns and bits of ocean, valleys and hills.

It *was* a map, like Abren had said. Mad Dog picked out Devil's Bridge. He picked out Aberystwyth. He even found the Rheidol and traced its path through the harbour out to sea, then looked the other way and traced it back up to the place from which everything on the entire piece of paper, parchment, linen or whatever it was, radiated like the hub of a giant wheel.

Plynlimon Mountain.

Somewhere behind him, Mad Dog heard Abren say, 'What *is* this thing?' Thing, she called it this time. Thing, not map.

Mad Dog put his face up close to it, looking for a clue. A smell came off, which he'd smelt somewhere before. For a moment, incongruously, it was the smell of boiled cabbage. Sharply Mad Dog found himself drawing in his breath.

'What's the matter?' Phaze II said.

Mad Dog shook his head. 'It can't be,' he said.

'Can't be what?' Phaze II said.

'*It isn't possible*,' Mad Dog said.

'What's not possible?'

Mad Dog stared at the map, and all sorts of memories came into his head, starting with the smell of cabbage and ending in the conservatory with the smell of candlewax and a man at a piano.

'Of course!' he cried out. Suddenly it all made sense.

Beyond the kitchen, he could see the windows of the conservatory. They were dark now, but once they'd glowed with candlelight and in it the Manager's tattoos had glistened like a road map drawn in blood. That was what Mad Dog had called it at the time.

'*A road map drawn in blood*,' he said out loud.

The sailors stared as if they didn't understand. 'This isn't a map,' Mad Dog explained. 'It's the Manager's tattoo.'

'It's his *what*?' they said.

'*It's his skin*,' Mad Dog said.

He stepped back, physically repulsed. The sailors stepped back too. The thing on the ground lay between them all, old beyond years; old and yellowing like a piece of parchment, or a snake's discarded skin.

'But *why*?' Mad Dog said at last, breaking their long silence. 'Why would anyone do a thing like this – tattoo a mountain and its rivers all over himself? I mean, look! It's everywhere. And it covers everything. There's the Gap, and there's No. 3. And there's Devil's Bridge and the Falls Hotel. Look, there's even Old Hall, where the old ladies live, who rescued me. And the crossroads between valleys, and the ruined cottage where my parents spent the last night of their lives. But why would anyone do a thing like this? Their entire skin, from head to foot, covered in the high roads, low roads and mountain rivers of Plynlimon. And why, having gone to all that trouble, would they leave it behind? It makes no sense.'

Phaze II shook his head. It made no sense to him either. But Abren shook her head because it *did* make sense. Perfect sense, she said – and she was shaking with anger.

'It's obvious,' she explained. 'Don't you see? This is his way of telling us he owns it. Plynlimon, I mean. By charting the mountain on his skin, he thinks he's staked his claim to it. All its woods and roads and mountain glens – he thinks they're his. And its rivers and their journeys to the sea. He's had them drawn up in his blood, Red Judge that he is, according to a law of his own making. And his claim is indisputable, or so he thinks, because this tattoo here is their title deed.'

She shivered. A little bit of night breeze got up behind her. It came rustling across the hotel garden, fetching the first few leaves of autumn down from the trees and blowing them across the lawn. Dust flew up between the kitchen and the cliff, and the map trembled, caught up in it all. For a moment it seemed to hover, inches above the ground, then it started breaking up and there was nothing any of them could have done to stop it, even if they'd wanted to.

Suddenly, like a snowstorm, a thousand tiny flakes of skin filled the air, swirling round and round. For a moment the air was thick with them, then the wind died down and it was as if the title deeds to Plynlimon Mountain had never existed. The flakes disappeared, every last yellowing little bit of them. Then leaves rattled along the ground again, and dust blew over the place where the map had lain, leaving nothing behind, not a single tattooed line.

Mad Dog stared at the bare ground, afraid to speak for fear of what might happen next. 'This *is* over, isn't it?' he whispered at long last. 'He has really gone this time? This really is the last of him? *Promise me that nothing like this will ever happen again.*'

Abren put an arm round him. She closed her eyes and said she wished she could, but, 'There'll be other people,' she said, 'other places, other seesaw struggles for possession and control. It isn't only here that these things happen. They happen everywhere – battles for land and wealth and people's sense of who they are. The world is full of it. It's full of managers and conjurors, tricksters, thieves and judges red in tooth and claw. But at least the struggle's over for Plynlimon Mountain. And down here on the Rheidol, it's over too. The mountain's free, and so are we.

'*So let's live like it, shall we?*'

30

Silver River

Mad Dog didn't know the first thing about living as if he was free but, that night – sitting through the long hours until dawn with Aunty, Uncle, a sleepy and thoroughly confused Elvis and the sailors – he made a first stumbling step towards it, opening up the dark places in his life and bringing out his secret stories one by one.

By morning, every last thing he could tell about himself, his past, his memories, his family and his fears, the things he'd done, the things he'd failed to do and even his hopes for the future had all come spilling out. Beyond the windows of the vardo, the birds started singing and sunlight heralded the new day. But, in the little living room, Mad Dog was too tired to notice. He could scarcely keep his eyes open and couldn't sit upright any more.

The sailors, who'd been telling stories too, weren't much better, saying that all they wanted now was to return to the hotel and find their beds. Uncle said that after a night like this, full of strange stories and even stranger lives, he needed bed as well – not just to sleep, but to spend a few hours on his own getting his head around some of the things that had been said.

But Aunty said she had a business to run and there could be no bed for her. It might be Sunday, and everybody else's day of rest, but there'd be guests wanting breakfast before too long; crises in the kitchen that only she could deal with; old arrivals who needed signing out and new ones needing signing in; even friends and family needing phone calls to assure them that Mad Dog really was all right after yet another of his disappearances at the campsite.

Mad Dog slept all day, awoke for Sunday afternoon high tea – which was a special occasion at the Falls Hotel – then slept again, not waking until the following morning when he found a newly labelled school uniform laid out at the bottom of his bed and realised it was time to face yet another change in his turbulent life.

He couldn't have felt less ready for the new school that awaited him, but faced it in true Trojan spirit. The key, he decided, pulling himself into his new clothes, was to put into practice what Abren had said about living as if he was free. Running wild on lonely mountaintops wasn't all that freedom was about. Sometimes it was about thinking hard thoughts and making hard choices. And that was what he was doing now, picking up his new school bag and allowing himself to be driven down to Aberystwyth to start something that, if he gave it a chance, he just might like.

And his first day in the new school was better than Mad Dog expected. He returned home full of news about the number of playing fields, the rugby cups on the wall, the size of the art block, the sheer scale of the library with all its books and computers and the dizzying array of fellow pupils and teachers whose names all had to be learnt.

Aunty, in turn, had news about the sale of No. 3, which she'd put on hold, until they'd had time to talk about it properly. And the sailors had news too, having done a bit of hard thinking and choosing of their own – and now stood, coats on, ready to depart!

Mad Dog felt as if a bucket of cold water had been thrown over him. Where were the sailors going, he demanded to know. And *why* were they going? How could they do this to him? Didn't they know that their lives were bound with his? The three of them together, Plynlimon's children, breathing the same air, and growing old together. They couldn't leave, he said. Didn't they know that? And surely, after all they'd been through – all the stories they had shared, and the things they'd faced together – they wouldn't *want* to leave!

The sailors tried explaining that being children of Plynlimon didn't necessarily mean hanging to the mountain's skirts, as if afraid of growing up, and being bound together didn't mean staying together all the time. The way they put it sounded worthy and excusable. They said that it was possible to be as close-knit as a family and yet still live separate lives.

But Mad Dog failed to be impressed. Beneath their fine-sounding words, he reckoned, the real truth was that the sea had got to them. He could smell it on them, and smell a new adventure far beyond the rivers of Plynlimon, and hear its siren call.

They were off for fun, weren't they? Off to their boat, harboured at Aberystwyth, thinking only of themselves. Anger welled up in him. The sailors promised they'd be back, but he felt betrayed. When they tried giving him a farewell gift, he thrust it back at them, saying he didn't need any more porcelain teacups, thank you very much.

But it wasn't cups the sailors were trying to leave

behind this time. Again they pressed their gift on Mad Dog, insisting that he should have it. And this time he took it – but refused to open it.

'I'll leave it until later,' he said.

'If you do that, you may regret it,' the sailors said.

Finally Mad Dog was persuaded to open the beautifully packaged little gift, tearing off the wrapping paper to find a silver necklace inside. *A silver chain necklace stuffed full of charms!*

Mad Dog dropped it, as if it was on fire. 'You must be joking!' he cried out. 'I don't want it. Take it back. You promised me. It was over. *Over* – that's what you said!'

Abren picked up the necklace. She said that it was over, but that didn't mean there weren't still things that needed laying to rest. Mad Dog asked her where they'd found it, and she said on the ground, the night of the map, but that they hadn't mentioned it before because the time hadn't been right.

'And now's right?' Mad Dog said. 'You're all ready to leave, and I'm left behind, and you call this *the right time*?'

Abren held out the necklace, but Mad Dog backed away from it and not even her insisting that it was a trophy, won in battle, fair and square, made any difference.

'You're the victor here,' Abren said. 'You're the boy who set Plynlimon free. So, by rights, this trophy's yours.'

Again she held it out, but Mad Dog didn't want a trophy any more than he wanted the necklace. Besides, it didn't look like a trophy as far as he was concerned. It looked horribly like what Aunty had once called a *poisoned chalice*, and how could he forget all the trouble the last poisoned chalice had brought into the family?

'If you're right and this *is* a trophy,' he said, 'then it can't just be for one of us at the others' expense. We're *all* inheritors here, not just me. The three of us are victors, which means you can't go off and leave me. There's a job here that needs doing, and we've got to do it together. This necklace has to be taken back up Plynlimon, where it belongs, and buried deep in the darkness where *it will never see the light of day again*.'

The sailors' departure was put on hold for one more night. Aunty allowed herself to be persuaded to lend them her Range Rover and a torch and a spade. Uncle wasn't very happy about it – especially as it was a school day in the morning – but Mad Dog showed him the necklace, saying that not for a single night did he want it in the same vardo, hotel or even village as him. And there was something about it that set even Uncle shivering.

It was getting dark by the time Mad Dog and the sailors were ready to leave. Phaze II drove. Abren sat by the window looking out into the night, her expression tight and faraway, as if it cost her dearly to return to Plynlimon. And Mad Dog sat between them, trying to feel safe but knowing he never would, not as long as the silver necklace weighed down his pocket.

They drove as far as they could by road, Mad Dog directing them until he no longer recognised where they were, and then Abren directing until eventually even she admitted she was lost. A gate appeared ahead of them, with a cattle grid beyond it. She jumped out to open it and a vast wilderness stretched out before them. Phaze II cranked the Range Rover into gear and they set off across it, heading directly into the heart of Plynlimon.

'When are we going to stop?' Mad Dog asked.

'When it feels right,' Abren said.

'What does that mean?' Mad Dog said.

'It means that we want to make sure it stays buried,' Abren said.

Mad Dog shivered. He remembered late-night horror films that he'd seen on the telly when Aunty and Uncle were still working, and the curious ways of vampires and ghouls, who always sprang back to life in the final frame. Phaze II asked what he was thinking and, when he told him, burst out laughing. He used to watch those sorts of films too, he said.

'But they're just stories. Their purpose is to scare you. This is different because it's real. And, in this story, we're in charge. What we bind here will stay bound. What we end here will be over, now and always.'

By now, the way had become so rocky that Phaze II could drive no further. He abandoned the Range Rover and they took to foot, wading across streams, climbing up sheep's paths and struggling through patches of bog. Eventually they came upon a stretch of open grassland that Abren seemed certain lay directly between the *ffynnons* of Plynlimon's three great rivers.

'Here's what we've been looking for,' she said, grabbing the shovel and digging out a first turf. 'Here, can't you feel it? This is the right place. Let's dig, shall we?'

It was a beautiful night – far too beautiful for digging but they gathered round, with bare hands and the shovel, and got stuck in. The ground was soft and peaty, but the task was far more difficult than they'd expected. Even shovelling out huge clumps of earth made no difference. No matter how deeply they dug, or how quickly, their holes kept filling with black, peaty water.

It was like trying to dig in a sea bed – only a thousand times dirtier. Soon Mad Dog, Abren and Phaze II were covered from head to toe in mud. They sat back on their heels, looked at each other and burst out laughing.

'Are you sure you got the right place?' Phaze II said.

'Are you questioning my judgement?' Abren said.

'I'm questioning your geography,' Phaze II said.

Abren flicked peat at him, and he flicked her back. Above them, the stars were out and the moon was a great peach-coloured disc rising regally over hills and mountaintops. Mad Dog looked up. It was the first time he'd witnessed a clear night on Plynlimon and the sky was huge and wonderful. On one side of it he could make out the orange glow of Aberystwyth. On the other, he could see the richest, deepest, most luscious black. And in between – arching right over Plynlimon Fawr – he could see another sort of light altogether, which wasn't starlight or moonlight or made by any city.

'What's that?' Mad Dog said.

The sailors stopped larking about and looked where he was pointing. Above Plynlimon Fawr, a sheet of what Mad Dog could only describe as lightness seemed to hang across the air, shimmering and shifting like the reflection of a landscape in a lake.

Abren wiped her eyes. 'It's the Aurora Borealis,' she

said. 'It has to be. Northern Lights, to you. A beautiful sight, isn't it?'

With a sigh, she turned away and started digging again. Phaze II said it couldn't be the Northern Lights, not this far south. Abren said of course it was, and they started larking about again.

Mad Dog left them to it and sneaked away, wondering what moonlit madness had got to them.

'Hey, where do you think you're going? Come back here!' Abren called.

Mad Dog replied that he wouldn't be long. He climbed a bank that rose immediately behind them, and started walking along the top, his head tilted back. It was years since he'd seen so many stars, going right back to when he'd been a little boy living on the road, when his dad had taught him the constellations, shape by shape, and told him all their names.

Mad Dog wheeled round for three hundred and sixty degrees, recognising shapes again, their names coming back to him. There was Orion, and there were the stars that formed its belt. There was its buckle and there, brighter than the rest, was Sirius the Dog Star. There was the Plough, sometimes also known as the Great Bear. And there, high above everything else, following a clear line drawn across the sky, was the great North Star around which everything radiated like the hub of a great wheel, or a Plynlimon in the sky.

Mad Dog could have stood there for minutes, hours, days or weeks, feeling the sky circling over him and the mountain beneath. What did time count for, caught up in a thing like this? Finally he started walking again, ending up at that string of ponds he'd discovered on his school trip. The first was still full of cotton-grass and the second of lily pads. But the third pond – the crystal-clear one, where he'd stopped to drink – was now so full of water that it was bursting its banks and flowing off across the moss in a series of silver streams.

'What's happening here?' Mad Dog said.

He picked his way down to the pond, which was as silvery as the moon. Across the moss, he could see its streams finally joining together in one single strand of water that shone as if it had been polished, even lighting up the sky. That he'd found the source of the reflected light over Plynlimon Fawr, Mad Dog had no doubt. But what was the cause of all this water, spilling everywhere like molten silver? Where did it come from? And where did it go?

Mad Dog looked out across the moss to the place where the land and sky were so bright that they became blurred and it was hard to tell one from the other. A shiver ran through him, as if he knew what he was about to discover. Knew too that, out there somewhere on the edge of this extraordinary mountain, all the answers to his questions awaited him.

Mad Dog left the pond behind and started heading for the shining strand of water, following the path of the criss-cross silver streams. Brightness pressed in on every side and he found himself almost blinded by an excess of light. He walked until finally he could go no further, standing on a grassy hilltop with a drop beneath his feet and nothing but sky ahead. And there, before his dazzled, unbelieving eyes, the single strand of shining water launched itself – out across space.

As if Plynlimon was its *fynnon*, it simply flowed away!

Mad Dog cried out. Before him, the single strand of shining water journeyed regally across the sky. It looped around the moon. It cut a path between the planets. It flowed amongst the stars, finally fading out of sight. And it was his mother's silver river. The one he'd missed the night that he was born. *Mad Dog was seeing it with his own eyes.*

How long Mad Dog stood there, he didn't know. All he knew was that he'd found the river that had given him his name. Found the treasure too, that the Ingram sisters had told him about. No wonder the Manager had wanted to keep it to himself and make Plynlimon his! With a secret like this, who wouldn't feel possessive?

Suddenly, as if something had finally slotted into place, Mad Dog found himself digging into his pocket and pulling out the necklace. What was it the Ingram sisters had said about people going up Plynlimon and never coming back? He held the necklace up in the light and its charms clamoured, as if struggling to break free. Every one of them was shaped like a tiny person, and there were hundreds of them hanging from the same heavy chain. Every one was different and had a different face, and Mad Dog found himself rifling back through them all, his heart pounding as if he knew what he'd find.

Sure enough, there they were at last – a little silver man, frozen in time with a bottle in his hand and a little silver lady with hair flying round her like a cloak of darkness. They could have been anybody because they were so small and their faces so indistinct. But

Mad Dog would have known his parents anywhere, made of any substance and at any size. They were holding out their hands to him – and Mad Dog understood at last why the sailors had said the necklace was his.

They'd known, hadn't they? They hadn't simply dumped this necklace on him, but had discerned its true nature and known what he'd find. Perhaps they'd recognised something from Mad Dog's description of his parents, or perhaps they'd understood anyway. But, either way, in agreeing to help him lay this necklace to rest, they had taken upon themselves the role of undertakers.

Mad Dog cupped the tiny figures in his hands. It wasn't for funeral services that he'd come back up Plynlimon. It wasn't for burials. If he'd thought it was, he'd got it wrong. He might have failed to rescue his parents once – and lived in shame because of it – *but he could rescue them now*.

Holding the necklace carefully, Mad Dog inched as close as he could get to the place where mountain and sky went their separate ways. Before him, he could see the silver river making its long journey between the stars. There were colours in that river that he'd never seen before and for which he had no names. Standing on the edge of the world, he watched them twisting, winking and flowing away. Once his mother had seen this river too, and raised her arms to it and wished that she could make its journey hers.

And now it lay in her son's power to make that wish come true.

Mad Dog threw the necklace as far as he could. It arched over the river and its chains burst open. A thousand silver charms started raining down. One by one, they struck the river's surface and were carried away. And a thousand silver sighs – including those of Mad Dog's parents – whispered *thank you* and *goodbye*.

31

The Most Noble Form of Travelling

Afterwards Mad Dog sat on the edge of Plynlimon, as close as he could get to the immense expanse of space, knowing that the mountain's treasure was his for the night. The river flowed away from him, looping over Plynlimon Fawr, almost touching it before cruising on over other mountaintops like the fiery tail of an enormous comet, and finally flowing away, leaving the earth behind and heading for the moon and stars.

But, for all that it was magical and utterly mysterious, it was a real river too – as real as any Rheidol that Mad Dog had ever called his friend. As it disappeared across the sky, Mad Dog watched fish leaping in its silver waters and kingfishers darting down them along with swans and herons, dabs and ducks, dipping cormorants and tall-necked geese, all heading off towards the stars as if theirs was an ordinary journey on just an ordinary night.

The entire river, it seemed, teemed with life. There were even boats on it, to Mad Dog's astonishment. When the first went past, he couldn't quite believe his eyes. There were even people in those boats. Ordinary people just like him. It was incredible. How had they got there, out on that water? And where were they going?

Mad Dog waved, and the people waved back and clapped their hands at him as if they knew about the silver necklace and were saying *good for you*. Mad

Dog couldn't have felt prouder if a procession of strangers kitted out in red-and-white had stopped to raise their feathered hats to him, or an army of soldiers to raise their standards and helmets.

The river carried them past in dinghies, sailing barges, tugs, trows, rowing boats and even tiny coracles, crewed by every sort of person from the youngest child to oldest man. Their boats were decorated with ribbons and the people called out to each other, laughing like kids on a school trip, and singing snatches of song that burst upon the night, only fading as they disappeared.

But one song didn't fade – and that was the song of the river itself. At first Mad Dog thought that another boat must be coming along, bigger than all the others, because the sound had the power of a distant ocean. But no boat came along, and the sound only grew, and it was then that Mad Dog realised that the river was making its own music.

The song that Mad Dog heard that night was unlike anything he'd ever heard. As he sat there, drinking it all in, the river swelled like an orchestra. It soared like a choir. It opened out its lungs like an opera diva full of arias. Caught up in the air, Mad Dog heard a hint of blues, a hint of salsa, a whiff of jazz bands, rock bands, gospel choirs and string quartets.

The river's song was a lover's croon. It was a folk singer's ballad, brooding and sweet. It was a child's lullaby. A soul sister's funk. Every type of music Mad Dog had ever heard, and every type he was yet to hear, was wrapped up in that song. Caught up in it, Mad Dog could hear electric guitars, tambourines, drums, whistles, cellos, clarinets, piano accordions, backing vocalists – even air guitarists playing in hope. Yet there was nothing discordant about it. All those different sounds, yet nothing was off-key. Nothing clamoured to break free. Nothing was the prisoner of anything else. Everything worked together perfectly.

Mad Dog laughed out loud. How could he not? This was a song of joy for open roads – a traveller's song for wide horizons and journeys without maps. For new adventures waiting to be had. For uncharted territories and taking risks. For never knowing what would happen next.

By now all the boats had disappeared, one after another like floats on a carnival parade. But Mad Dog knew that if he lived to be a hundred and spent the whole time adventuring, he'd never witness a more noble form of travelling. What a river this was, he thought to himself. What a king and queen of rivers! What a mother, father, sister, brother, aunty and uncle of all rivers!

'Anything could happen on a river like this!'

The voice behind him put the words into his mouth. Mad Dog turned around to find the sailors standing behind him.

'*Anything*,' he agreed.

No sooner was the word out than one final tiny boat came bobbing along, completely empty as if waiting for a crew. Mad Dog took one look at it and knew what would happen next. Sure enough, the boat began to detach itself from the main thrust of the river, cutting back against the current and heading for the shore.

Mad Dog watched its progress, knowing that it was coming for him. His mouth went dry and his heart began to pound. All he had to do, he realised, was wait until the boat was close enough, then wade out to it and climb on board. It was easy. It didn't take Trojan blood to do a thing like that. Didn't take his mother telling him that he'd always be a rover, or that he should trust in the power of the open road.

But, as the boat continued to come closer, Mad Dog broke out in a sweat. Was this something he should do, or was it something he'd regret? What would happen if he got in that boat, and where would it take him? Who would he become, and what would he have to leave behind?

The boat continued to bob his way until it was close enough to almost touch. Here it danced on the spot, impatient to be gone. The sailors waded out to steady it, then turned back towards Mad Dog as if expecting him to be behind them, waiting to climb on board.

But Mad Dog held back. It wasn't fear of adventure that caused him to hesitate, or lack of readiness for the journey. Faced with leaving them, it was the people that he'd never see again. He had a brother, didn't he – a brother who, if he went, would have no one left from his old life. Then there were his friends to think about – Hippie, Luke, Rhys and all the rest of them. Then there were Aunty and Uncle. Once they'd wanted to adopt him because they loved him, they said, and he hadn't believed them, but now he did.

Besides, Mad Dog thought to himself, he'd promised to never run away again, and maybe Aunty and Uncle weren't that hot at keeping promises themselves, but they'd always done their best for him and clearing off like this seemed a poor reward.

The boat bobbed, increasingly impatient to get

away. The sailors struggled to hold it steady but Mad Dog told them not to wait.

'Go *without me*,' he said.

The sailors looked astonished, as if they wouldn't dream of it, no matter what they might have done only a few hours before, back at the hotel – not on a journey of this magnitude. But Mad Dog had known, from the moment he'd turned round and seen them there behind him, how things would end up. It had been obvious even before the boat had come along. In fact it had been obvious years ago, if he stopped to think about it, sitting round the fire at No. 3, the sailors saying, 'But there *is* no journey's end. That's what we've discovered. All horizons lead to new ones, all discovery to even more.'

'Go,' Mad Dog said. 'I mean it, *go*.'

The sailors didn't need to be told a third time. Mad Dog watched them helping each other into the boat. He wished that he could go with them but understood what held him back and knew he'd made the right choice.

'One day,' he said, wading out to them, 'I'll bring the others with me and we'll catch you up. At least I hope we will. I'll do my best.'

He reached the boat but didn't get in. The three of them looked at each other as if they understood that there'd be no surprise returns this time – no storms to bring them back together, and definitely no possibility of postcards. Mad Dog dug through his pockets, wanting to give the sailors something to remember him by. At first he couldn't find anything but then his hand pulled out a crumpled feather that had once looked white but now, in the extraordinary light given off by the river, shone like silver.

Mad Dog smoothed it out. He'd made the right choice here, as well. Red stood for blood and earth and tattooed maps and things that had to be possessed. It was the colour of the Manager. But silver was the colour of the river – and it was Mad Dog's colour too.

'Here,' he said. 'Once, someone gave me this. Now you take it.'

The sailors took the feather just before the little boat started moving away. For a moment it trembled as if the greatness of the journey ahead just might overwhelm it. It looked small and vulnerable, like a nutshell about to be caught up in a mighty flood.

'Don't you worry about us,' the sailors called. 'This isn't the first time we've gone off into the unknown. We'll be all right. We always have been and we always will. Goodbye, goodbye. We won't forget you.'

'*You'd better not*,' Mad Dog called back. Then they were gone, swept up in the main thrust of the river, and the last he saw of them was a silver feather, shining like a beacon to point the way.

Long afterwards, Mad Dog stayed on. The sun broke over the hills and the silver river was shot through with gold. Mad Dog watched it shining right across the sky. Then it faded with the stars, and he mightn't have known what became of it, but here where it arose – here on the mountain where he'd lost his parents, and found a treasure, and heard a song that he hoped one day to hear again – Mad Dog felt the river heal him.

Everything was made right by it. Everything. And, more than right, it was made *good*.